The stakes of this "game" are too high for *any* player.

As fast and quietly as I could manage, with my hands shaking so violently they could hardly aim the key, I shoved it back into the keyhole. If someone had wanted my key out so their key could unlock the door, as I suspected, they'd find they couldn't get away with it.

My key hit against something hard, and I thought I heard someone on the other side of the door grunt in surprise.

I waited for the person to try to dislodge my key again, but it didn't happen.

Was someone still there? Had he left when the key trick hadn't worked? Or, with all the noise of the thunder and wind, had I just imagined what I thought I'd heard? Maybe no one had been outside my door at all.

I was scared to death, but still so curious I couldn't stand it. I slid out my key and bent down to peer through the empty keyhole. Lightning lit up the sky, and in that sudden white-bright flash, I saw the gleam of an eye looking back at me.

JOAN LOWERY NIXON

THE NAME OF THE GAME WAS MURDER

LAUREL-LEAF BOOKS

Published by
Bantam Doubleday Dell Books for Young Readers
a division of
Bantam Doubleday Dell Publishing Group, Inc.
1540 Broadway
New York, New York 10036

ISBN: 0-440-21916-7

RL: 5.7

Reprinted by arrangement with Delacorte Press

Printed in the United States of America

December 1994

10 9 8 7 6 5 4

OPM

To Louise Hagen
my sister-in-law and friend
with love

ONE

I clung to the heavy oak door for support, terrified of the old man seated behind the cluttered desk. His gargoyle eyes—magnified by thick, overlarge lenses—were huge, wet shimmers in a pale, shiny-bald head; and he hunched into a tight, stoop-shouldered ball as though at any minute he'd fling out moldy wings and swoop toward me. "What do you think you're doing here?" he snapped.

As long as I could remember, Augustus Trevor had been famous as one of our country's greatest literary novelists, and he was almost as well known for his well-publicized socializing with kings and presidents and a lot of people with tons of money. I had expected to meet the Augustus Trevor with the charming smile and elegant manner—the one I'd seen in so many photographs—but the Augustus Trevor who glared at me from behind his desk was a much older, scowling, mean-tempered person, and I was shocked.

I tried my best to smile but couldn't make it, and I began to sweat. Whether it was from nerves or because of the heat from the smoldering fire in the huge fireplace behind him, I didn't know. "I—I'm Samantha B-Burns," I stammered.

"I didn't ask *who* you are," he snapped. "I asked what you're doing here."

Good question. I was beginning to wonder myself, but I took a deep breath and started over. "I'm here because I'm Aunt Thea's niece. That is, my mother is her niece."

His scowl didn't waver, and I wondered if he understood who I meant. "Thea, your wife," I explained. "I suppose I should have waited for her to introduce us, but I couldn't wait to meet you. You're the reason I'm here. I mean, I've heard a lot about Catalina Island and Avalon, and the great beach and the music, and 'island of romance' and all that, but *you* . . ." His face was crinkling like a dark purple prune, so I quickly added, "but the main reason for my coming is *you*, Mr. Trevor."

His lips parted, and he made a kind of burbling sound, the way babies do before they spit up, so I thought I'd better explain a bit more. "I asked Aunt Thea if I could come for a visit before school begins in September, because I'm pretty sure that I'm going to be a writer, but I don't think I can do it without help, and I've brought some stories . . . I'd be so grateful if you'd read them and tell me if I really have any talent and give me some advice."

It was awful trying to talk to someone whose face was screwed up in agony. "Remember?" I asked quickly, and smiled encouragingly. "Two years ago I mailed you a story I'd written, and I really didn't expect you to answer. I mean I did then, but I don't now because I realize the story wasn't terribly good. I was only thirteen then, but I've been writing something every day—an article in a writers' magazine said to do that if you want to be successful—and, as I said, I've brought these stories. . . ."

Augustus exploded from his chair and scuttled around his desk. "Stop that foolish prattle!" he screeched.

I realized that he was short, too, and that surprised me. It's hard to think of a literary giant as short, but Augustus Trevor was definitely short. I'm five six, and we were facing each other nose to nose.

Still maintaining a tight grip on the edge of the door, I mumbled, "I know I talk too much when I get nervous, and I'm really nervous meeting you, Mr. Trevor."

"Then go home," he said.

"I can't," I told him, although at the moment I wished with all my heart that I could. I hadn't just asked to come. I'd begged Mom and Dad. I'd pleaded. I thought about what Dad had said about how I always jumped into things without thinking, and I had to admit that in this case, at least, he'd been right.

I suddenly realized that Augustus had regained control of his emotions and was speaking to me, so I took a deep breath and tried to pay attention.

"Young lady," he said, "I invited you to leave. The correct response would have been 'I will,' not 'I can't.' What do you mean by saying 'I can't'?"

"I mean that because I was coming here my parents decided to take a trip they've always wanted to the Grand Cayman Islands. That means no one's home, and Mom would really be mad if I went home and lived there alone for two weeks, only I couldn't anyway, because I've got one of those nonrefundable airline tickets and not enough money to get another one, and then there's the matter of food, because all I've got is spending money and . . ."

Augustus grimaced as he reached out and grabbed me, his bony fingertips digging into my arms. "I have better plans than entertaining you," he said. "I am hosting a house party this coming weekend for some very important people, and you'll be in the way."

"Aunt Thea didn't tell me about the party," I answered.

"Thea didn't know about it."

"Maybe you should have told her," I suggested helpfully, and tried a smile. "You can't blame Aunt Thea for telling me I could come and visit, if she didn't know you'd planned something else." Augustus scowled again, and I quickly added, "Look, I'll stay out of the way while your party's going on. I promise. You won't even know I'm here."

And after your guests have left, then maybe you'll be used to having me around, and you'll read some of my stories, I thought, *because if you don't, how will I know if I can really be a writer or not?*

Augustus let go of my arms, and I rubbed them as he stood there silently, looking as if he was thinking over what I'd said. Finally his pupils, swimming like fat fish in goldfish bowls, focused on me. "What room did Thea put you in?"

"It's a big room," I told him. "It's got a huge bed with a dark red spread and canopy and red carpeting and French doors that open onto a balcony."

"I suppose you'll have to remain on the island, but you can't sleep in that room. It's reserved for Buck Thompson."

"Buck Thompson? You mean Buck Thompson the network sportscaster? That guy who does all those shoe commercials with little kids?"

Augustus's only answer was a sneer of disgust in my direction. He strode toward the fireplace and yanked on a long, thin piece of tapestry that hung on the wall next to it. I knew what the tapestry was because I'd seen bellpulls like that in old movies. It was an odd, old-fashioned contrast to the modern computer that sat on his desk.

Suddenly a voice spoke behind me. "Yes, Mr. Trevor?"

I hadn't heard anyone approach, and I jumped, whirling to face a slightly plump woman who wore no makeup and whose streaked gray hair was pulled back tightly and knotted at the base of her neck. She was dressed in a navy blue cotton dress with a high neck and long sleeves and looked exactly like what she probably was—a housekeeper.

"Mrs. Engstrom, this is the daughter of Mrs. Trevor's niece," Augustus said, leaving off my name as though it weren't important. "Due to Mrs. Trevor's carelessness in not asking my plans, this young woman will be our house guest for a brief period of time. She has been wrongly assigned to the Red Room, so please remove her things and escort her to the tower room at the end of the south wing."

I smiled at Mrs. Engstrom, but she didn't smile back. She gave me just the briefest of glances and said to Augustus, "The tower room is quite small and off to itself, Mr. Trevor."

"The other bedrooms will be occupied. Take her things to the tower room," he said with emphasis. "That will be all, Mrs. Engstrom."

She nodded and turned, and I quickly followed.

Augustus Trevor was the most disagreeable, obnoxious dork I had ever met; and it made me angry that people read his written words that rippled and tumbled and fell like beautiful waterfalls one on top of the other, and thought that because he wrote super-wonderful stories he must be a super-wonderful person. It wasn't fair.

I had to trot to keep up with Mrs. Engstrom as I followed her across the massive entry hall with its large black and white diamond-shaped tiles, careful not to trip on the edges of the oriental rugs that were scattered over the floor. We went up the sweeping, carved stairway, the sound of our footsteps lost in the heavy carpeting, and turned left, hurrying down the hall to the Red Room. There was no sign of Aunt Thea.

"Which is Aunt Thea and Uncle—uh—Mr. Trevor's room?" I asked Mrs. Engstrom.

"Your aunt's room is the one nearest the head of the stairs," she answered. "Mr. Trevor's is directly across the hall from the room we are in."

"Oh," I said, and felt my face grow warm. I gathered up my suitcase and backpack, glad that I hadn't unpacked them, and again followed the silent Mrs. Engstrom down the hallway, which was dark in spite of the wrought-iron sconces, each of which held clusters of small, low-watt light bulbs.

She stopped outside the last door and threw it open, then stood to one side. Instead of the room I'd expected, I saw a narrow, curving flight of stairs. "It's just a short flight," she told me, "but the stairs are steep, and my knees aren't what they used to be. If you don't mind, I won't follow you."

"I don't mind," I said, and smiled at her again. "By the

way, my name is Samantha Burns. Everybody calls me Sam."

She nodded, but she didn't smile in return. What a household! At least Aunt Thea seemed to be glad I was here.

I shifted my suitcase into my other hand and edged into the stairway.

"I'm sorry," Mrs. Engstrom murmured. I twisted around to tell her not to be, but she was on her way down the hall.

I wondered just what it was she was sorry about. Sorry that I had to clump and squeeze my way up this weird stairway? That I'd had to change rooms? That Augustus Trevor was a mean-minded nerd?

The stairs made only a half circle and ended at an equally narrow door that was arched on top. A large brass key protruded from the keyhole. Feeling something like Alice in Wonderland and hoping I wouldn't shrink, I turned the key, pushed open the door, and entered the tower room.

It was perfectly round, including the part of it that was partitioned off for a tiny bathroom. Inside the room there was only enough space for one twin-size bed, a small chest of drawers, and a chair. I dropped my suitcase and backpack on the bed and walked to the narrow windows that ringed the outer curve of the room. Beyond, in the distance, lay the sea, but the view was marred by the bars set into the stone.

I rested my forehead against the glass and groaned. In spite of gentle Aunt Thea's presence in this house, I was beginning to get scared. "I can't believe this," I said aloud. "I'm in prison!"

TWO

I needed to get out of that room as soon as possible, so I unpacked in a rush, tossing my journal and stories, my shorts and T-shirts and other stuff into the empty drawers. Mom had insisted that I bring two dresses, so I hung them in a tiny makeshift closet I found in the bathroom and threw open the door of my bedroom.

I stopped with my hand on the doorknob, the cold brass key touching my fingertips, and for a moment I stared at it, a peculiar chill shivering around the back of my neck. While I was inside the room, with the door closed, anyone could have turned that key and locked me in.

Stop that! I told myself. *It's not just a key. It's an ornament . . . maybe an interior decorator's attempt to try to carry out a theme in this yucky castle. Big deal. Nobody locks doors inside a house.*

But it didn't matter what I'd told myself. How could I know what people did in Augustus Trevor's house? I grasped the key and turned it in the lock, feeling it grind and grate until there came a deep and final click, then shoved the key into the hip pocket of my jeans and took off down the winding stairs. I had to talk to someone—anyone. I needed to hear a human voice.

Unfortunately, that "someone, anyone" didn't include my parents.

You know how awful it is when you tell your mom and dad you have to do something, and they tell you all the reasons you shouldn't, and you say they're wrong, only they turn out to be right.

"Take it easy, Sam," Dad had told me when I insisted how important it was for me to visit Aunt Thea and meet Augustus Trevor. "You've always been like this—the minute you get an idea you want to rush right into it. Slow down and think this out. If you want to be a writer you can be one. You don't have to depend on Augustus Trevor's help."

"Thea has never invited us to her home," Mom pointed out, and I thought I could detect a slight trace of bitterness as she added, "I wouldn't doubt that her celebrity husband has been responsible for that."

Aunt Thea had visited our family a few times, and we'd enjoyed her visits. She went shopping with me for a really hot jacket, took me to the best beauty shop in town for a terrific new haircut, and taught me how to play cribbage. But Augustus had never come with her, and we'd never been invited to visit them. If it was Augustus Trevor's fault, I honestly didn't blame him. If you could have lunch with the Duke and Duchess of Kent and dinner with Robert Redford, why would you want to hang around with the Burns family of Elko, Nevada?

"Augustus Trevor is one of the world's greatest writers.

He has to place a high priority on his privacy," I said, and winced at how stuffy I'd just sounded.

"Which is all the more reason that it wouldn't be polite to invite yourself," Mom had insisted.

"Don't you see?" I pleaded. "Ever since I decided that someday I'm going to be a writer, I've wanted to meet Augustus Trevor. If I'm in his home for a visit I can get his advice. He'll let me know if I really have writing talent or just think I do. Whatever he tells me can influence my entire career."

"As I remember, you sent Trevor one of your stories a couple of years ago," Dad said, "and he didn't bother to write to you about it or even return it."

"But this time I'd be there in person! Don't you see what a difference that would make?"

Dad gave me one of those looks, and I realized I was overdoing it, but Mom and Dad just didn't understand how much it would mean to me to be guided by Augustus Trevor.

Mom sighed and said, "I suppose you could call Thea and ask if she'd want you to come for a visit. If it wouldn't be convenient, I'm sure she'd be honest enough to say so."

I made the call and started to talk to Aunt Thea about all sort of polite nothing stuff, but I couldn't stand waiting to ask my question and get the answer, so I blurted out, "Aunt Thea, could I come and visit you for two weeks?"

For a few seconds there was only silence. My face grew hot, and my hands began to sweat, but finally Thea said, "Of course you can visit us, Samantha. I'd love to have you as a guest."

"Thank you, thank you, thank you!" I shouted, and

Mom took the phone away from me to chat with Thea and talk about travel arrangements.

Three weeks later Aunt Thea met me at the Los Angeles airport, and we took a taxi to the harbor. We were ushered aboard Augustus Trevor's launch by a couple of crew members and were soon on our way to Catalina Island. His own launch! Wow!

I said something about being eager to see Avalon and the beach, but Thea looked surprised. "Oh, Samantha, I'm sorry," she said. "Our home is on the opposite side of the island, past the Isthmus, and rather remote from the Avalon area, I'm afraid."

"That's all right," I said. "I don't mind hiking it."

She shook her head softly. Everything about Thea was soft, from her pale gray-blond hair, through her light untanned skin, to her eyes that looked like reflections of the washed-out blue of the sky. "We're not connected to the road that runs through the island," she said. "Our only transportation is by boat." Thea gently brushed back a strand of hair that had blown across my eyes and smiled. "Don't look so disappointed, Samantha. We'll see that you get a glimpse of Avalon. We'll take you there in the launch."

Just getting a glimpse of Avalon wasn't quite the same as lying on the beach in my new blue bikini, hoping the lifeguard would notice it was the exact same shade of blue as my eyes. My best friend, Darlene Barkholter, spent two weeks on Santa Catalina Island a year ago, and I heard plenty about the lifeguards at Avalon, who were real hunks. I can't say I hadn't given the lifeguards some thought.

Darlene and I have always been interested in the same

things, from the time we met in third grade. We shared a tree house, wrote countless letters to each other in code all the way through fifth grade, and joined the same clubs in junior high and high school; so I would have shared Darlene's appreciation of the Avalon lifeguards. However, I reminded myself that the reason for my trip wasn't to enjoy watching lifeguards. I had a much more important, literary purpose, so I assured Thea that I didn't mind missing Avalon at all.

She began telling me about something called the Santa Catalina Island Conservancy, which was a foundation formed to preserve the natural resources of the island, and how someday Augustus's 1920s island house would belong to the foundation, but I'm afraid I didn't pay much attention. I relaxed and looked out at the deep blue water and the sky in which clumps of clouds were beginning to gather, their edges darkening like watercolors that had run together. I let the ocean spray sting my face, and I thought about how someday I'd love to have an island home and a boat just like this one. Maybe, someday after *I* became a famous writer.

Catalina is just twenty miles off the coast of California, so it didn't take us long to arrive. We swung north, went around the far tip of the island, and docked behind a motorboat at a short, covered pier in a small, narrow cove. One of the crew from the launch carried my suitcase and backpack up a steep, winding stairway to the house, while Thea and I followed.

What a house! It was so weird that I wondered for just an instant if I'd wandered onto the set of a Halloween horror movie. Spread out, with corridors rambling in all directions, this ugly stone castle sat alone on a scrubby hill covered with a thick tangle of sage and short golden-brown grasses under wind-twisted oak trees. Beyond were higher hills, blurred purple-blue with mists, and from where we stood we had a picture-postcard view of the sea.

Thea had led me to a large bedroom and said she'd leave me to unpack. I guess I should have stayed there and waited for her, but the moment she had left I went downstairs in search of the man I was so eager to meet, the famous author Augustus Trevor.

That had been a big mistake.

Now, as I walked down the staircase to the landing, my footsteps muffled by the thick carpet, I took my time, listening intently for the sound of another human being; but the house was silent. For the first time I paid attention to my surroundings. From my vantage point on the landing I could look down on the immense entry hall and get a good view of part of the living room as well, and I was amazed to see that the house was cluttered with museum-like stuff. Besides all the heavily framed paintings on the walls, there were wood carvings of animals and people, all kinds of big and little statues (some of them pretty weird), glazed pottery bowls, china plates, and even a crystal bear which sat on a table near a window. Souvenirs from their travels? Gifts from royalty?

As I turned away from the railing my attention was caught by a pedestal which was tucked into the deep angle of the landing. A burnished gold vase with a rounded lid stood on the pedestal, and I stepped closer to examine it. The vase was close to two feet high and about ten inches in diameter, with a wide base. It was graceful and curved and heavily ornamented with designs and markings that looked like scrunched-up little faces.

I reached out my hand to touch the lid, but someone spoke close to my ear, startling me. I jumped and the vase wobbled, but I caught it in time.

"Are you looking for something, miss?"

I turned to see a tall man dressed in dark pants and a white jacket. He was staring down at me with a bland, noncommittal expression, and I'd seen enough British-made television programs on PBS to recognize immediately that he must be a butler.

"I'm Sam," I said. "Samantha Burns. Thea Trevor's niece. I was just looking at this vase."

"That is not a vase, Miss Burns," he said. "It is a burial urn."

"Oops." I took a step away from it. "You mean somebody's in there?"

"Not to my knowledge," he said. "Considering that the urn dates back quite a few centuries and has undoubtedly traveled through many hands, I would assume that by this time it is empty."

That was not a pleasant thought. Somebody thought his ashes would be tucked away in the urn forever, and what happened? Someone carrying the urn tripped? Opened it in a windstorm? Dropped it through an open carriage door? Gross! If my ashes had been lost so carelessly, I'd be angry enough to come back and haunt my urn.

I took another uneasy step away from it. "Mr. uh—uh—"

"My name is Walter," he said.

"Walter, that urn isn't haunted, is it?" I asked.

"I believe there is some sort of legend to that effect,"

Walter answered, "but you will have to ask Mr. Trevor about it. I do not believe in ghosts." He became more businesslike as he added, "Is there anything I can do for you?"

"Yes," I said as I shot another uneasy glance toward the urn. "Can you tell me where my aunt is?"

He gave a slight nod and answered, "I'll take you to Mrs. Trevor. She is in the sun-room."

There was a sun-room in this house? Great! Did that mean a hot tub? An indoor pool? Things were beginning to look up. I trotted down the stairs after the butler and followed him across the entry hall toward the back of the house.

The sun-room was formal and just as overdecorated as the rest of the house, but it did have large windows framed by sheer curtains and heavy drapes. The windows overlooked an uneven landscape of grasses, low shrubbery, and wind-twisted oaks which led steeply down to the sea. Aunt Thea was seated in a heavy wicker chair, her back to the window. Clouds had dimmed the sun, but there was enough brightness left to outline Aunt Thea with an aura of pale green light.

As I came in she looked up and placed a delicate china teacup on the silver tray which rested on the low table in front of her. "Samantha dear," she said, "I'm sorry that you met Augustus so abruptly, without warning. He can be a little frightening, if you aren't used to him."

"It was my fault," I told her. "I couldn't wait. That is, I mean, he's so famous, and he's such a great writer, and I know you would have made the introduction easier." I shrugged and added, "Dad keeps telling me I jump into things without stopping to think."

She smiled. "Impulsive is the word."

I smiled back because I really liked Aunt Thea. As I flopped into a chair I stretched out my legs and sighed. "Impulsiveness says it all. I guess that's something I'm going to have to watch out for in my writing. There's so much to learn."

Aunt Thea reached over and patted my knee. "Be patient with yourself. Becoming a published writer takes years and years of practice and experience. Do you think that Augustus had immediate success?"

Her question caught me by surprise. "Why, yes," I said. "He did, didn't he? His first book won that big literary award and boom!—instant fame."

"His *fourth* book," she said. "The first three were rejected many times over."

"They were?" I mumbled, and tried to absorb what she'd said, but Thea changed the subject.

"I'm sorry, too, that Augustus moved you to the tower room. I know it's small and unhandy, but since he'd assigned the other rooms to his guests—"

"Please don't apologize," I interrupted. "The tower room is a really—uh—interesting room. I—uh—like it."

Thea paused a moment, accepting what we both knew was a polite fib, then picked up a teacup in one hand and a silver teapot in the other and asked, "Would you like a cup of tea, Samantha?"

"Oh . . . yes, thank you," I answered. I'd rather have had a soft drink, but I supposed tea was okay if it had a lot of sugar and lemon in it. Thea handed me a cup and saucer, and even though I was still bemused by what she had said about Augustus's rejections, I noticed there was another cup and saucer on the tray. "Is uh—Mr.—I mean, is your husband going to join us?"

"Why don't you just relax and call him Augustus?" she suggested.

"I—I don't think I could do that."

Aunt Thea took a sip of tea and nodded. "You'll soon begin to feel comfortable with him."

I seriously doubted that, but I didn't have to say so, because Thea went on to explain, "The extra cup is for Laura Reed. She arrived this morning, and she'll be down to join us at any minute."

"Laura Reed!" I nearly dropped my cup. "You don't mean Laura Reed the movie star, do you?"

"The very same," Thea answered. "She's one of Augustus's guests for the weekend party he planned."

"He didn't tell you about the party before I got here," I said, but Thea just shrugged.

"Augustus has always been able to bring home unannounced guests and know they'll be well cared for."

I put down my cup and leaned forward. "Aunt Thea," I said, "I didn't mean to crash his party. I'm sorry if I caused any trouble."

She smiled as she reached out and squeezed my hand. "Don't look so worried, Samantha. You're not the cause of any trouble. Augustus tends to be hotheaded when things aren't going the way he's planned, and during the last few years the painful bouts he's had with arthritis and gout haven't helped his disposition. But I'm sure you'll find that he'll be perfectly charming while you're here. He can be a very gracious host when he wants to be."

Easy for her to say. She hadn't had him throw a temper tantrum right in her face.

Or had she? I got the uncomfortable feeling that she wasn't telling me the truth.

"Hello, Thea."

I rose to my feet as Laura Reed—the famous movie star Laura Reed—glided into the room. Maybe I expected flashing lights and little twinkle stars and a mink coat and a sparkly sequined dress. I didn't expect what I saw: a pretty but quiet woman who wore no makeup. Her blond hair—just a shade lighter than mine—hung straight and heavy around her face, and she was dressed in a simple white blouse and navy blue jeans.

They had to be designer jeans, I told myself as Aunt Thea introduced us. And the blouse—she probably bought it on Rodeo Drive. After all, Laura Reed was a movie star, so she must have a ton of money, in spite of the fact that her last two movies had bombed.

She took both my hands and looked into my eyes as she smiled shyly. Shyly? A movie star? She reminded me more of a mouse. "I'm so very pleased to meet you," she murmured in a voice all sleepily whispery and throaty.

"Thank you," I answered. "I'm pleased to meet you, too."

I was excited at meeting Laura Reed, and one part of my mind was already thinking about what I'd tell Darlene: *Laura? Oh, she was nice. Very friendly. And it's true, her eyes really are a kind of greenish-gold.*

But another part of my mind was registering the fact that there was an odd expression in those eyes. What did they remind me of? She was looking at me, talking to me, and yet she wasn't. I mean, I could see that her mind was somewhere else, and it must not have been a very happy place, because she was nervous. I wondered if Augustus

Trevor's weird house was having an effect on her. Burial
urns, tower rooms with bars on the windows—if I opened
a closet door and discovered a mummy, I wouldn't be in
the least surprised.

Laura had seated herself, so I quickly sat down too,
picked up my cup, and tried to sip as nonchalantly as
Laura and Thea.

They chatted for a few minutes, mostly about old
friends and old parties. I didn't know most of the people
they were talking about, and I was a little disappointed
that things weren't turning out to be as exciting as I hoped
they'd be. My attention began drifting away, but it
quickly returned when Laura put down her cup and
asked, "Thea, you must tell me. Why am I here?"

Aunt Thea's eyes widened. "Why are you here? I don't
understand, Laura. You were invited to Augustus's weekend party, and you came."

Laura shook her head impatiently. "Party? I'd hardly
call it a party."

"But Augustus said . . ."

Laura Reed sighed and leaned back against the plumply
cushioned sofa. "Obviously, *you* don't know either."

"Know what?" Now it was Thea's turn for impatience.
"Laura, please explain what you mean."

"Very well," Laura said. "Augustus wrote, asking me to
be here. No. He didn't ask. He *told* me to come. He said
there would be a game in which I'd be one of the chief
players. His exact words were, 'If you don't take part,
you'll soon regret it.' " Laura leaned forward, her golden
eyes trained on Thea like piercing spotlights. "I came because I was afraid to ignore his threat."

Thea paled. "You must be mistaken, Laura," she said. "Surely, Augustus would never threaten his friends."

"Friends?" Laura whispered. "I'd hardly say we were friends."

I thought about what Laura had told us, and I had to agree with her and not with Aunt Thea. What Augustus Trevor had written to Laura Reed sounded like a threat to me.

THREE

The tea party was uncomfortable, with Thea trying to be a gracious hostess, in spite of what Laura had told her, and Laura trying to be a charming guest, even though it was obvious she'd rather be anywhere else. To ease the situation they both turned to me.

"You're lucky to lead a normal life," Laura said, and patted my hand. This time her smile was wistful, and her words dragged, plopping themselves down like reluctant feet. "You'll never know what it's like to . . ."

"To be rich and famous?" I offered helpfully.

"To be used," she corrected. "To want to be really loved —not as a star, but as a child, hungry for affection."

I wasn't sure how to answer her, but I needn't have worried because she rambled on about the traumatic people who had affected her adult life, from parents to hairdressers. Thea and I just listened. I stopped being embarrassed by Laura's revelations and began thinking that I'd have a lot of really interesting stuff to tell Darlene.

Even though it was midafternoon, the room gradually became darker, and finally a maid in uniform came in, turned on some lights, and began picking up the empty cups. She had a round, cheerful face, and looked as if she might be only a few years older than me.

Thea went to the window. "It looks as though it's going to pour," she said. "Such odd weather for August."

The maid stopped, tray in hand, and said, "Mrs. Trevor, the radio news said there's going to be a storm. It's part of a hurricane moving north from Mexico."

As she spoke she looked at Aunt Thea with a kind of pity and tenderness. It was obvious that she was fond of Aunt Thea, but I didn't understand why she should pity her.

"Thank you, Lucy," Thea said. "I didn't listen to the radio today. I wasn't aware of a possible storm."

Radio? What about television? It dawned on me that I hadn't seen a single TV set in this house. Two weeks without television? It was hard to imagine.

Thea sat down again and announced, "The launch just pulled up to the dock, which means the other guests have arrived. We'll all be snug and cozy before the storm breaks."

Snug and cozy in this creepy old castle? I didn't believe it.

Laura sat up stiffly and asked in her kind of choking, breathy way, "Who are the other guests?"

"Augustus told me that Buck Thompson is one of them," Thea said.

I eagerly volunteered, "You know who Buck Thompson is, don't you? He used to be a pro quarterback, only now he's a sportscaster on one of the networks." I realized that

I shouldn't have interrupted, so I quickly said, "Sorry, Aunt Thea."

Thea just smiled at me and continued. "And Julia Bryant will be here."

"Julia Bryant!" I blurted out.

Thea raised one eyebrow and said, "I take it that you're familiar with Julia's books, Samantha, although I'm a little surprised that you'd like that type of novel."

"I really don't," I answered, and blushed as hotly as one of Julia's female characters. "I mean, this girl at school was talking about one of them, and she read a couple of scenes to us, and they were kind of wild, but I read some of the rest of the book, and it was boring."

Laura nodded vigorously. "You're right. Julia's novels are sleaze. They're drivel. And the last one on television was badly cast. I was up for the part, but then someone got the idea of casting this twenty-two-year-old with absolutely no talent . . ."

"More tea?" Thea asked, and held the teapot toward Laura as she said, "I'm sure you know that when Julia's novels began making the best-seller list she set up a foundation to help support budding novelists—all in the name of an old friend."

"What a neat idea," I said, and could just see myself doing something like that in Darlene's name. Or maybe I'd put both our names on it. "I bet that made her friend happy."

"Thea should have said *in memory of* her friend," Laura told me. "Julia's friend wanted to be a writer and, as I heard it, wrote dozens of manuscripts, but never had enough courage to send them to a publisher."

"What happened to her friend?"

Laura sighed. "Apparently, she destroyed all her manu-scripts, then jumped out of a twelfth-floor window."

"How awful!" I said.

"There's no point in going into any of the arts unless you have a dedication and determination to achieve," Laura began, then suddenly changed direction as a thought struck her. "Will Julia's husband be here too? You know Jake, don't you? The poor boy never was able to make it as an actor, even though he's a *very* attractive man."

"Augustus didn't invite him," Thea said, and looked embarrassed as she tried to explain. "He didn't invite Senator Maggio's wife either. That's United States Senator Arthur Maggio of Nevada."

"Has anyone else been invited?" Laura asked.

"One more guest," Thea answered. "Alex Chambers."

I'd heard the senator's name often enough, since we lived in the same state, but I was a lot more interested in the dress designer, Alex Chambers. His clothes were high-class expensive, in tons of magazine ads, and it was a good chance that if Laura Reed was wearing designer jeans, *Alex Chambers* was the name on the label.

There was silence for a moment, until Laura murmured, "I wonder if each of your other guests received the same kind of threat I did."

"Oh, Laura, now really," Thea began, but Laura turned the full wattage of her green-gold eyes on Thea and said, "We're supposed to be players in a game. I just wonder what the game is going to be."

Aunt Thea informed me that we would dress for dinner, so I went up to my room and put on a dress and a long string of Venetian glass beads that Darlene had given me for my birthday. I wondered why anyone who chose to live on an island would want to dress up and live in a castle with maids and butlers, when it made a lot more sense to wear shorts and go barefoot and live in an open, comfortable house where you could clean up by just sweeping the sand out the front door every morning.

I decided that if I became a famous writer, I'd do exactly that. Of course, at the moment I didn't know if I should try to become a writer or not. I was depending upon Augustus to tell me.

We were all supposed to gather downstairs for cocktails at seven, and I wasn't about to go down early all by myself, so I stood by the window and watched a swarm of dark clouds battle the sun, which struck out with shards of red and gold before it was smothered and dragged toward the sea.

The gloom was so intense that I turned on the bedside lamp. I sat on the edge of the bed, where I could keep one eye on the clock, and pulled my journal and a pen from the top drawer of the chest. The writers' magazines I read suggested that writers and would-be writers keep journals and write something in them every day. I had no problem with that because I like to write.

I wrote what I had thought about the sun, but that didn't lead anywhere, so I decided to write a description of the room I was in. Only I went even further and added some cobwebs and dust and the sound of something creeping up the stairs.

At the loud knock on my bedroom door I screeched, threw my journal into the air, and jumped to my feet.

"Are you all right, Miss Burns?" a muffled voice asked.

I staggered to the door, turned the key and opened it. "I'm fine, thank you," I told Walter. There was no way I was going to explain. He'd think I was pretty weird.

Walter looked at me as though he thought I was pretty weird anyway and said, "The guests have gathered in the front parlor, Miss Burns. Your aunt would be pleased to have you join them."

I had been so interested in what I'd been writing that I'd forgotten to watch the clock. "Okay," I said. "Thanks." I watched Walter descend the stairs before I locked the door. I hefted the big brass key in my hand, trying to decide what to do with it. My dress didn't have a handy pocket to hold it.

Inspiration struck, and I opened the clasp on the string of beads, ran the string through the large hole in the middle of the key, and fastened the clasp at the back of my neck. At least I'd have my key with me. I wasn't going to leave it in the door.

The long upstairs hallway was dim and deserted, except for me, and I hurried along, nearly running, because I had the awful feeling that someone—or something—was watching me. I practically galloped down the stairs, pausing only for a few seconds on the landing to glance at the burial urn, which, even in the shadows, seemed to glow.

"Listen, whoever you are," I whispered, "my name is Samantha Burns, and I'm an innocent bystander. I had nothing to do with your urn or your ashes, so if the scary feeling in this house is coming from you, please . . . leave me alone!"

I didn't wait for an answer. I certainly didn't want one! I just ran down the rest of the stairs and joined the lights and noise in the front parlor.

The room was festive with dozens and dozens of glowing candles and bowls of bright summer flowers. I began to relax and enjoy myself, especially after Aunt Thea—comfortably soft and gray in a cashmere knit dress the same shade as her hair—took me by the hand and introduced me to Senator Maggio, Alex Chambers, Buck Thompson, and Julia Bryant. I was in famous company!

Each of the guests smiled brilliantly in my direction and told me they were pleased, quite pleased, very pleased, or terribly pleased to meet me. Julia Bryant did remark on my necklace. "How exciting and unusual! That darling antique key looks so authentic and—hmmm—somehow familiar. Wherever did you find it? Neiman's?"

"No, in my door," I said, "and I don't really think it's an antique, because doesn't something have to be one hundred years old before it's called an antique?" Trying to make polite conversation, I continued. "One of my mother's friends has an antiques store, and she finds some of the most unbelievable things in . . ."

I stopped talking because they hadn't been listening and had gone back to their conversations. I even lost Aunt Thea as Julia put an arm around her shoulders, drew her into the semicircle she'd created with Alex and Laura, and said, "Thea, you must hear about the fantastic charity ball that our dear, generous Alex is underwriting."

I wasn't interested in Alex Chambers's charity ball, so I wandered away from the groups and stood alone, watching them. People-watching is good practice for anyone who wants to be a writer, according to my writers' magazines.

Buck Thompson's face was familiar. It would be to anyone who watched a pro football game on television. He was huge and beefy, his face tinged dark red like a medium rare steak. His hair was brown, thick, and unruly. It was Buck's own hair, not a toupee, so I'd have to tell Dad his guess was wrong. Buck's movements were overlarge and expansive. As he spoke with Senator Maggio, Buck just missed knocking a flower arrangement off a nearby table.

I'd seen Senator Maggio's face in the newspapers. Because he was round and bald I never thought he looked like a senator ought to look—especially one who's being considered as a possible presidential candidate. But he was well groomed. He wore a dark blue suit made out of some silky fabric, and he carried his head high. I wondered if he'd ever had a P.E. teacher like Mrs. Tribble in ninth grade, who kept saying, "For good posture, pretend there's a string at the top of your head, girls, and it's pulling, pulling, pulling you upward."

A laugh tinkled like broken glass, and I turned toward the sound. Laura, in a long, plain gown of deep blue silk, her hair brushed out in a golden glow, looked softer, younger, and prettier in the candlelight. Again she laughed, but the brittle sound told me that she was every bit as wary and nervous as she had been earlier.

Julia had dressed like a twenty-year-old model in kelly green satin, with a skirt hem high above her knees and a low-scooped neckline. Her hair was dyed red, and she wore layers of makeup. If Darlene were here, she'd agree with me that it didn't help Julia Bryant to try to look young. She had to be at least fifty. "No. What you heard was wrong. I'm just an old-fashioned girl," she was saying. "I'm not the least bit mechanical-minded and hate having to use computers."

Alex Chambers smiled from one woman to the other. "You should try computerizing designs," he said. He was tall and slender, with wisps of dark hair and large brown eyes which blinked a lot when he wasn't squinting. I bet he wore glasses when no one was around. He had on tight slacks with a twisted rope holding them up, instead of a belt, and a silk shirt the color of whipped cream. The shirt was buttoned only halfway up, but the opening was filled with a knotted, bright, multicolored scarf.

People-watching was interesting for only so long. I wandered over to a large round table in a nearby corner, which was cluttered with dozens of photographs. In each of them Augustus Trevor—mostly young or middle-aged —was buddy-buddy with someone who looked important and official. I recognized Prince Rainier of Monaco and the Shah of Iran, but the others were unfamiliar.

As I picked up an ornate silver frame, Mrs. Engstrom appeared beside me. She carried a small tray of canapes, but she seemed more interested in the photo in my hand. "That's Mr. Trevor with the late King George the Sixth of England," she said. With her free hand she pointed to one photo after another. "That's King Juan Carlos of Spain, the late king Gustav Adolph of Sweden, King Fahd of Saudi Arabia, the late king Frederick the Ninth of Denmark . . ."

"They're all royalty?" I asked.

"All of them," she said. "In fact, Mr. Trevor calls this 'the Kings' Corner.'" Mrs. Engstrom's mouth had a strange twist to it, as though she thought this was putting things on a little too much.

As Mrs. Engstrom moved on to pass the canapes to the

other guests, Lucy came into the room with a tray of assorted drinks and handed me a glass of ginger ale.

"Thanks," I said. Eager for someone to talk to, I asked, "Where's Mr. Trevor?"

"He'll be along," she said quietly, and glanced back at the open doorway. "He likes to come in after everybody else has been standing around waiting for him."

I wanted to ask more about Augustus Trevor, but Lucy left, delivering drinks to the other guests. Walter was busy too, so I was trying to decide whether to stand by myself, looking stupid, or stand with one of the groups, looking stupid, when Augustus Trevor entered the parlor. Conversations stopped in midsentence as we all turned toward him. In the silence a gust of wind suddenly rattled the windows, and I wasn't the only one who jumped.

Augustus looked like a character in one of the old movies Mom and Dad like to rent. He was casually dressed in a dark red velvet jacket with a belt that tied around his pudgy middle. Augustus also wore dark slacks and loafers without socks, and smiled charmingly at his guests. "How delighted I am that all of you could come," he said, and made a little bow. "Welcome to our humble home."

Laura gave a sigh, as though she'd begun breathing again, and Senator Maggio cleared his throat. Julia was the first to come forward. She clutched Augustus's shoulders and blew smacky kisses near both ears.

"You darling man, I've been so excited. What *is* this wonderful imaginative game you've thought up for us?"

I saw Buck and the senator glance knowingly at each other, so that answered one question. Each of these guests had received the same kind of invitation. *Threat,* Laura had called it.

Augustus chuckled and draped an arm around Julia's shoulders. "All will be explained when the game commences," he said, and went through the room greeting the other guests with the warmth of a gracious host. I could see what Aunt Thea meant when she had said Augustus could be charming when he wanted to be.

Augustus even had a smile for me, which made me instantly hopeful. When the weekend was over and his guests had left, he'd offer to read my stories and critique them. I *knew* he would.

But there was something even more pressing I wanted to ask him. "Tell me about the ghost," I said.

He stepped back, and his eyes bugged out, but he didn't answer, so I said, "You know, the ghost in the haunted burial urn. Isn't there some kind of legend?"

Augustus's eyes narrowed. He hunched forward and grabbed my shoulders as he growled in my right ear, "There's not only a legend, it also has a curse with it. It's as simple as this: Stay away from that urn or there will be nothing left of you."

"That's not a very nice legend," I mumbled, and squirmed out of his grip.

"It's not a very nice ghost," he snapped, and hobbled over to talk to the senator.

What a crab! His charm didn't last long, as far as I was concerned. I felt sorry for the ghost and hoped he'd give Augustus Trevor a bad time.

The dinner was interesting, since I was never quite sure what had been served. There were purple and yellow crunchy things in my salad—things that aren't too common in Elko, Nevada—and the thin slices of meat rested in some kind of creamy sauce with a red design drizzled around the edges. There were rows of forks at the left and one above the plate, but I stopped trying to figure out the silverware and menu so I could listen to the celebrities and what they had to say.

The earlier mood of caution and suspicion had faded, and everyone talked and laughed a lot. Senator Maggio and Buck, who sat across the table from each other, compared notes about bloopers they'd made in high school football, and somehow the senator worked the conversation around to grandchildren and brought out some pictures of two fluffy-dressed little toddlers. He beamed when he talked about the little girls, but since Thea seemed to be the only one interested in them, his grandfatherly bragging didn't have much of a chance.

Julia, who was seated next to the senator, sparkled as she discussed book tours and confessed to sneaking under a fence to get away from a pair of excited fans. Laura, on my right, tried to top Julia's stories by telling us about some of her harrowing experiences on movie sets.

It was fascinating to me to see some of the celebrity glow peel away like banana skins, giving a glimpse of real people inside; and I wondered if these people often hid inside protective skins so no one could guess their thoughts and feelings. I was just a beginner at this people-watching business, but it was obvious to me that Augustus was the only one who was any good at being famous.

Julia, the author, was like an actress playing the role of one of her sophisticated fictional heroines, and yet at times she looked unsure of herself, and I saw her watch the others questioningly, as though she wasn't quite sure they were taking her seriously. Buck, who sat at my left, was just as nervous—maybe even more ill at ease. He grabbed a spoon to finish off the sauce, then dropped it and turned red when he saw me watching him. And now I knew what the expression in Laura's green-gold eyes reminded me of: our neighbor's dog's puppies who wiggled and yipped and looked up with huge, begging eyes at everyone who came in sight, as though they were saying, "Love *me*. Oh, please, love *me*!"

Senator Maggio, no longer a doting grandfather, had become controlled and polished again; and Alex never dropped his smug conceit. Both of them were safe inside their banana skins, and I wondered what it would take to make them come out.

It had begun to rain, not a soft rain or even a steadily tapping rain. It came in bursts with the wind, whipping against the window like small stones, and I was glad none of us had to go outside in that storm.

We had just polished off a tart filled with fresh mixed berries and soft vanilla custard, when Augustus's voice boomed out. "Please give me your attention, my friends. I have an important announcement to make."

FOUR

Buck's water goblet went over, and water sloshed on the table as he grabbed for it. Julia giggled nervously, and Laura sucked in her breath. We all waited quietly as Augustus resettled himself in his chair before he continued.

"As you are all well aware," Augustus continued, "I am a novelist. I have never been interested in writing nonfiction." He paused and smiled. "Until a little over a year ago."

As we waited, none of us knowing what we were supposed to say, Augustus chuckled. "For the past thirty years," he told us, "I have been thoroughly involved in high society's self-centeredness and hypocrisy. It suited my purposes, and occasionally it provided characters and ideas for my stories."

"Oh, my, I knew it. Prince Rainier," Laura murmured. "Was he the basis for—"

Augustus leaned forward with a scowl. "I have not finished speaking," he thundered, and Laura cringed against the back of her chair.

Augustus was silent for a moment, and when he spoke again it was with a smile. "My current manuscript is not another novel. It is a book in which I intend to make public certain shocking behind-the-scenes behavior of a great many very important people."

Julia stiffened, and it was obvious that she couldn't keep silent, no matter how offended Augustus might be. "Are you telling us that we're included?" she asked.

Augustus grinned nastily. "Yes and no," he said.

"What is that supposed to mean?" Buck demanded.

"It means that while doing background research and interviews, in an attempt to supplement my notes and refresh my memory, I stumbled upon a well-hidden secret in the past life of each one of you."

"Ridiculous!" Senator Maggio snapped.

"Oh, is it?" Augustus asked, and his eyes gleamed. "If these secrets are made known, they'll be damaging enough to ruin your reputations, aside from other complications that might result."

"This is absurd," Alex interjected, but Augustus dismissed him with a wave of his hand and went on.

"Each of you committed one very stupid mistake in your past, yet the mistakes were never made public. Was this because you were actually smart enough to cover them, or because you were incredibly lucky?"

"Augustus, I protest!" Aunt Thea said. "You're embarrassing our guests, and—"

"Sit down, Thea," Augustus ordered, and she did.

"You are all highly successful in your careers," he continued, "and normally that takes a certain amount of intelligence. So what is the truth? Are you stupid, or are you not? I'm going to find out. During the weekend we're going to play a game, and you'll be given clues to solve. The clues will lead to a significant treasure—a treasure that in itself will be self-explanatory.

"If you can solve the clues, then you'll prove to me that your stupid mistakes can remain secret, and I'll remove every trace of your stories from my manuscript. For those who can't solve the clues, the world will soon learn the shocking facts from your past."

"This manuscript you're threatening us with—have you written it or are you simply threatening to write it?" Alex demanded.

"Oh, I've completed it," Augustus answered. "It's ready for its final revision before I send it to my agent, who will proceed to read it immediately and send it on to my publisher. In its current form, your mistakes are detailed."

"Where is this manuscript?" Buck asked. He scowled from under his heavy eyebrows, and his anger was so strong that for a moment I was afraid.

But Augustus wasn't. He leaned back and smiled. "Violence won't accomplish what you want, my dear Mr. Thompson. Clear and sharp thinking will."

Buck hunched over in his chair and grumbled, "I don't know what you've got in mind, but you won't get away with it, Augustus."

Suddenly Senator Maggio shoved back his chair and got to his feet. Tiny lines at the corners of his eyes twitched, and his lips were so tightly pressed together, they were pale. "I'm leaving," he said. "Your weekend game is simply an exercise in self-aggrandizement, Augustus, and I want no part of it. Will you please make arrangements for your launch to take me to the mainland?''

"I'm leaving too!" Julia announced, and jumped to her feet.

Everyone got up except Augustus, and even though we were all looking down at him, he still seemed to be the most powerful figure in the room. I think it was because he never stopped smiling that wicked smile, even when he was talking.

"The launch was taken to the mainland and docked there for greater safety during the storm," he said. "I hadn't counted on any of you being foolish enough to refuse to play the game."

"There's a smaller boat," Buck said. "Is that gone too?"

"No," Augustus said, "but you'd have to be quite desperate and somewhat mad to take a boat like that in choppy seas."

The senator must have faced tough opponents before, because he remained calm. "Then I'll remain in my room until the launch is able to return," he said.

He began to turn away from the table, Julia tentatively following him, but Augustus warned, "Just remember, if you leave this room you'll lose your opportunity to have your damaging secret removed from the manuscript. I prefer that you all return to your seats so the game may begin."

"I don't have any damaging secrets," Julia murmured, but she slipped back into her chair.

After a brief moment of hesitation the others followed her lead, even Senator Maggio. Me? I was one of the first to be seated. I didn't want to miss a thing.

Mrs. Engstrom brought in a tray of tiny macaroons and

bonbons and quietly poured demitasse cups of coffee, passing them to the guests, who were all so intent on Augustus, they ignored her.

Aunt Thea, who sat at the far end of the table, seemed paler than usual and close to tears. Most of the guests looked down at their hands or away at the windows, not wanting to meet another pair of eyes, but Alex shrugged, as if he were only going along with the gag as a good sport, and asked Augustus, "You said the clues would lead to some kind of treasure. Exactly what is this treasure we'll be looking for?"

"You'll know it when you find it, and you'll find it through the clues," Augustus said, and his grin became broader.

"Aren't you going to help us?" Laura whispered.

"Of course," he answered. He reached into a deep pocket in his velvet jacket and brought out six sealed envelopes on which names had been printed in bright blue ink. He read out the names, then passed the envelopes down each side of the table to the correct recipient. Even Aunt Thea got one.

"You might call this a warm-up to the game," he said. "Inside each envelope you'll find a personal clue. You can test your skills by seeing what you can learn from what you've been given."

Julia didn't hesitate. She ripped open one end of the envelope and tugged out the contents. "This is a clue?" she asked. "It's nothing but part of an airline schedule, New York to Buffalo."

"And I've been given a train schedule," Senator Maggio complained.

Alex held up an enlarged section of what seemed to be a

detailed map and said with a touch of sarcasm, "Maybe Augustus is suggesting the three of us plan a trip together."

"In Vietnam?" I murmured. I'd been able to read a few of the names on the map.

Alex did a double-take, stared at the map a second, then folded it and dropped it into his shirt pocket. He didn't answer my question. He wouldn't even meet my eyes.

"Study your clues," Augustus said, and hunched over, chuckling to himself like some evil gnome.

Shamelessly, I looked over the shoulders on each side of me. Laura was holding a list of football games and scores, while Buck stared at a list of names and telephone numbers. One was circled: Peeples, Willie.

Laura said. "You made a mistake, Augustus. These football scores must be for Buck. They don't mean anything to me."

But Julia suddenly gasped as she stared at her clue, and the senator, his face darkening, angrily folded his paper into a hard, tight square, and stuffed it into his pocket.

Thea suddenly spoke up. "Augustus, I don't want to be a part of this game."

He nodded toward her, giving a kind of bow, but he said, "Oh, yes you do, Thea."

"How could you?" she whispered. Tears came to her eyes, and her fingers trembled as she folded what looked like a travel brochure—I could read the word *Acapulco*—and tucked it back into the envelope.

"None of this makes sense to me," Laura said.

I reached for her clue. "Would you like me to help you?" I asked. "I'm really good at clues and codes and stuff like that. When we were younger a friend and I spent years making up crazy codes to solve."

I realized that I had the attention of all of them, but Laura didn't seem to notice and said, "Oh, thank you, Sam. If you can figure this out, I'll be eternally grateful."

"Figure it out yourself, Laura!" Augustus snapped. "That's the point of this experiment—to see if you're smart enough to save your own skins!"

"I'm sorry," I mumbled. "I was just trying to help."

"You want a clue?" he went on. "All right, Samantha, I'll give you a clue. In fact, yours may make more sense than all the rest of them." He pulled a scrap of paper out of his pocket and bent over it, hiding it as if he were taking a test, wiggling the fingers on his left hand, while with his right hand he wrote. When he'd finished writing, he folded it over and gave it to Laura, who passed it to me.

When I smoothed the paper out flat I saw a series of numbers and recognized a simple letter–number code that Darlene and I used way back in fourth grade: One stands for *A*, two for *B*, and so on.

7–5–20 12–15–19–20

Insult me with something like that, would he? I crumpled the paper into a wad and glared at Augustus.

The others had been watching, but Laura had been leaning over my shoulder. "Ohhh," she said. "It was written in code, and she figured it out so fast! She *is* good!"

"Perhaps I underestimated you," Augustus said to me.

"Perhaps," I murmured, and tilted my nose in the air until it occurred to me that I probably looked as conceited as Alex.

"Augustus, what did you mean, Sam's clue may make the most sense?" Julia asked.

Still angry, I didn't give him a chance to answer. "It doesn't," I said. "Why would he want to give something special to me? He was just kidding."

The rain increased with such force that when Thea spoke no one could hear her, and she had to repeat, "Augustus, what are we supposed to do now?"

Augustus propped his hands on the edge of the table, elbows protruding like chicken wings, and shouted, "It's late. I'd suggest you all retire to your rooms and meditate on the meanings you've found in your clues."

"What meanings?" Laura asked in a pitiful voice, but Augustus ignored her.

"There'll be another set of clues for you in the morning," he said.

Thunder slammed and rolled around the house, and I wasn't the only one who jumped.

"The storm may interfere with your sleep, but you won't have to worry about any loss of electricity," Augustus said. "We have our own generator."

Everyone began leaving the dining room, and I glanced toward Laura, whose bleak, miserable expression reminded me of the look that our school's halfback, Moose Munchberg, gets whenever he has to take any kind of test. Augustus had told me not to help Laura, and his glance was firmly on me, so I bypassed her, kissed Aunt Thea's cheek, and said good night.

Thea's skin was cold, and she clung to me for just an instant.

"I can help you," I whispered, "no matter what Augustus says."

But Thea shook her head and answered, "Thank you, Samantha. You're a dear girl, but I've already deciphered my clue. Better be off to bed. Breakfast will be served anytime after seven."

I passed Mrs. Engstrom at the dining room door. She stood as quietly and motionless as a mummy—her lips held in a tight, angry line and her eyes glittering in the dim light—so I started when I saw her.

"Good night, Miss Burns," she said.

"Good night, Mrs. Engstrom." I wasn't quite sure what a housekeeper did. Maybe she planned things. Maybe she took care of the cooking. Politely I said, "That was a very good dinner. I liked the . . . uh . . . chicken?"

"Veal," she said. "I'll tell the cook. Good night."

I hurried up to my tower room, eagerly turning on the light and locking the door behind me. The storm was really noisy up here, but in a way I kind of liked the whoosh and slam of the wind and rain. It slapped the walls and rattled the windows in a sort of rhythm, like waves crashing on rocks, while lightning slashed the blackness with blue-white explosions.

I decided to write that description in my journal, but when I sat on the edge of the bed, curiosity got the best of me, and I opened the crumpled wad of paper I was still holding.

I hadn't quickly deciphered it, as Laura had thought. I'd been too angry about the little-kid code. So now I took enough time to work out which letter went with which number and came up with the message: GET LOST.

Funny. Very funny. I didn't see a wastepaper basket, so instead of tossing the paper, I stuffed it into the pocket of my jeans, which were still draped across the bed.

Okay, I thought. *You want me to get lost? Then I will!* The minute the launch came back I'd leave the island, and tomorrow I'd ask Aunt Thea to lend me enough money to get another plane ticket home. I'd stay with Darlene and her family and refuse to let myself worry about what my parents would have to say.

I'd had all I was going to take from this horrible man with his crazy game.

FIVE

I didn't sleep very well that night, and I'm sure none of the others did either. The storm picked up in intensity, and—even with my down pillow wadded on top of my head—the noise of the wind and rain and thunder was incredible.

Was that the creaking sound of a door opening? I sat up in bed, clutching the blanket and sheet to my chin and listened as hard as I could. Footsteps . . . up the little stairs. Footsteps . . . coming closer . . . closer . . . closer. Was the doorknob turning? It was too dark to tell. As the key seemed to rattle in the lock I cried out, "Stop, or I'll shoot!"

A heavy blast of wind slammed against the windows, and I told myself I couldn't have heard soft footsteps under all the noise the storm was making. It had to have been my imagination. My face grew warm with embarrassment when I realized what I had just yelled. How dumb could I get? I must have heard that awful line while my parents were watching their old rental movies, and it

stuck in my head. Thank goodness I was off by myself
where no one could hear me!

But the key jiggled again just as lightning brightened
the room. I saw it. For an instant I think my heart stopped,
and my whole body turned cold. Footsteps or no footsteps, what was making the key jump like that?

I climbed out of bed and ran barefoot to the door, just in
time to catch the key as it tumbled from the lock.

Someone had poked it out of the door!

As fast and quietly as I could manage, with my hands
shaking so violently, they could hardly aim the key, I
shoved it back into the keyhole. If someone had wanted
my key out so their key could unlock my door, as I suspected, they'd find they couldn't get away with it.

My key hit against something hard, and I thought I
heard someone on the other side of the door grunt in surprise.

I waited for the person to try to dislodge my key again,
but it didn't happen.

Was someone still there? Had he left when the key trick
hadn't worked? Or, with all the noise of the thunder and
wind, had I just imagined what I thought I'd heard?
Maybe no one had been outside my door at all.

I was scared to death, but still so curious I couldn't
stand it. I slid out my key and bent down to peer through
the empty keyhole. Lightning lit up the sky, and in that
sudden white-bright flash, I saw the gleam of an eye looking back at me.

I screamed. I couldn't help it. And for a moment everything got blurry and fuzzy. My head buzzed, and I
thought I was going to faint. Luckily I didn't, because I
heard footsteps running away down the stairs and knew

whoever had come to my room had gone. What was the person after? I didn't have anything of value. Could it have been my clue? Did someone want to know what message Augustus had given me? I wished Augustus hadn't been so flippant about it. Someone probably had believed him when he said that my clue may have made more sense than all the rest of them.

Clutching the key tightly, I climbed back into bed. I knew I wouldn't sleep. I'd probably never sleep as long as I was in this house!

But at some point I opened my eyes and found that the thunder and lightning were off in the distance and the room had grown lighter. I checked my wristwatch and discovered that it was already eight o'clock in the morning. No wonder I was starving. I bathed and dressed in a hurry, pocketed my key, and hurried downstairs through those dim, gloomy halls, moving even faster as I passed old somebody-or-other's burial urn. I was eager to reach the dining room, which was bright with the light from the huge crystal chandelier. I didn't like being alone. I needed someone to talk to.

Unfortunately, no one else was there.

The table had been reset, and on the sideboard there was an array of covered warming dishes, bowls of strawberries and melon, platters of rolls and muffins, and small boxes of cereal. I was glad to find that this food was familiar, and there weren't any artistic sauces to confuse me, so I helped myself to some of everything except the cereal—I could have cornflakes at home—and sat down to eat.

"Good morning, Miss Burns. Is there anything else you'd like?" As she entered the room Mrs. Engstrom eyed my heaping plate, then walked to the nearest warming dish and peeked inside as though to reassure herself I hadn't taken *all* the eggs. "Please tell me if there's anything you need or if there is anything I can do for you. I want your stay here to be as comfortable as possible."

"Thank you," I said, and then I blurted out, "Mrs. Engstrom, I haven't told Aunt Thea yet, but I will as soon as I see her, and I'm telling you because you probably have to plan for how many there are at meals and all that . . ." I took a deep breath and tried to slow down. "What I mean is, I'm going home as soon as the storm is over and the launch comes back."

I expected her to nod formally, but instead her face softened, and she said, "Your aunt will be disappointed. She told me how much she was looking forward to your visit."

"But not everyone here wants me," I began, and uncomfortably shifted in my chair.

"Your aunt does and she's lonely," Mrs. Engstrom told me.

I nodded. "I'd be lonely too, if I had to live in this castle, away from my friends and the malls and all that. Aunt Thea and—and Aug—and her husband used to travel a lot, and I remember Mom talking about their town house in New York City. I don't understand why they decided to hole up here."

"Mr. Trevor has always come here to write," she said. "He demands complete quiet. When he's working on a book, no one—not even Mrs. Trevor—is allowed in his office."

I didn't mean to pry, but I was curious. "But what does Aunt Thea do to keep busy while they're living here?"

Mrs. Engstrom's lips tightened again, and she said,

"Mr. Trevor has never wanted to hire a secretary, so Mrs. Trevor has always done the job. She answers Mr. Trevor's mail. You wouldn't believe how much mail he gets. There's fan mail, and invitations to speak to various groups, and requests for donations—all sorts of things—and she takes all his phone calls, and watches out that he's not disturbed while he's working or resting."

"But what does she do for fun? I saw a cribbage board in Aug—uh—Mr. Trevor's office. Do they play cribbage? Read? Watch TV?" I sidetracked myself by asking, "There *is* a television set somewhere around, isn't there?"

"I'm sorry," Mrs. Engstrom said. "It's too difficult to get good reception here."

I wanted to ask her more about Aunt Thea, but Mrs. Engstrom's face had closed over, like someone pulling down a shade, and I had to admit to myself that I had no right to get nosy. "All right, I'll stay," I called after Mrs. Engstrom as she turned and moved toward the door.

She stopped and actually smiled at me, and I could see how protective she was of Aunt Thea. I guessed that the staff all detested Augustus and loved Thea, and must be here only because they were paid awfully well.

My mouth was full of hash browns when Laura Reed staggered into the dining room and flopped into a chair. "Coffee," she groaned. "There must be coffee around here."

I got up and brought her a cup of coffee. It was hot and black. She sipped at it for a few minutes, and apparently it did something for her, because she began to wake up. She sat a little straighter, took a deep breath, and looked to each side, twisting to peer behind her.

"Do you want something else?" I asked. "Breakfast is over there." Pointedly, I added, "It's a serve-yourself."

"I'm not hungry," she whispered, and leaned toward me, shoving a folded paper into my hand. "I just wanted to make sure that Augustus wasn't skulking around someplace. Honestly! The nerve of that man! He reminds me of the director on my last picture. Terrible personalities, both of them."

I opened the paper and saw that it was the list of football scores.

"You offered to help me," Laura said. "So help. Okay?"

"Augustus said . . ." Oh, who cared what Augustus had said. I scanned the list. "Have you tried to work it out yourself?"

Laura sighed. "Work out what? I didn't even read it. I don't know anything about football scores or what they mean."

"I don't know all the teams myself," I said. I checked the first of the scores to see if they were in that easy number-code, and they weren't, but maybe there was another kind of clue in one of the numbers. "I'll read the list out loud," I told her. "If anything seems familiar to you, just speak up. One of these numbers might be a locker number, or part of an old address, or something like that."

She nodded, and I began to read: "Final Scores: Rams 14, Buffalo Bills 6; Falcons 13, Oilers 21; Giants 6, Forty-Niners 7; Emerald Bay 1, Stars 0."

There were a lot more listed, but I didn't read them, because Laura let out a tiny, high-pitched shriek, sounding like a mouse being chased by a cat. She clapped her hands to her cheeks, gasped as though she were hyperventilating, and stared at me in terror.

"What happened?" I asked.

"Nothing!" she wheezed, and snatched the paper out of my hand.

"Something I read must have—"

"Never mind! Forget about it!" Laura jumped to her feet and ran out of the room.

She couldn't have worried that much about the scores. Was it the Emerald Bay and Stars teams that upset her? I'd never heard of either team, but then I wasn't that much of a football fan. I buttered a muffin and began to eat it. The people in this house were getting stranger and stranger.

By the time I'd finished breakfast Alex and Julia had come downstairs. Alex had dark bags under his eyes, and Julia looked terrible. The heavy makeup she wore hadn't helped a bit. I tried to make some kind of conversation with them, but Alex made it obvious that he didn't want to talk.

Julia seemed to like to talk about herself, so I said, "I couldn't believe it when Norelle died."

Julia peered at me over the rim of her coffee cup. "Who?"

"Norelle. In your *Sudden Surrender*. I watched it on TV."

"Oh," she mumbled, and then she said, "Oh" again as though she'd suddenly figured out who I was talking about.

"Why did you decide to have her die?"

"I—I guess it just seemed to fit the plot."

"Even though Prince Eric wanted to marry her?"

"Tough luck for him," she mumbled.

"Wait a minute," I said. "I was mixed up. Prince Eric wasn't in *Sudden Surrender*. He was in *Leftover Love*."

Julia seemed flustered, and a couple of drops of coffee

sloshed onto the saucer as she put down her cup. "Oh. That's right," she said.

I chuckled. "I can see how *I* could get mixed up about which of your characters were in which book, but it's funny that *you* would, too."

She didn't look too happy, so I searched my mind for something else having to do with writing. "When you were first starting out as a writer, did you get many rejections?" I asked.

She had just put her coffee cup to her lips, and she made a kind of funny sputtering sound in it. She managed to wipe off her mouth and chin before she turned and clutched my arm with one hand. Her long fingernails hurt. "What do you mean by that?" she demanded.

Alex had stopped eating to watch us, and that seemed to upset Julia even more. "Tell me," she snapped. "What do you mean?"

Startled, and a little bit scared of her, I tugged my arm away and slid my chair out of her reach. "I—I'm hoping to be a writer too," I said quickly, "and I need to know all sorts of things, and I don't have any writers at home to talk to. Of course, when I was in the ninth grade an author came to visit our school. She's one of my very favorite authors, and I love her books, but she told us that her first book was rejected twelve times, and then the thirteenth publisher—"

"Stop!" Julia cried, and clapped her hands over her ears. "I didn't ask for a history of your life."

"I was just trying to explain," I said. "The visiting author told us her husband encouraged her to keep trying. Did your husband encourage you?"

Julia put both hands on the table to steady herself and frowned at me. "Who put you up to this? Augustus?"

"Put me up to what? I was just trying to be friendly."

She studied me for a moment, then seemed satisfied and went back to staring into the bottom of her coffee cup. "I can't think this early in the morning, so no more quizzes. Haven't you got something better to do?"

"I'm sorry," I mumbled, even more embarrassed because I could feel myself blushing. I pushed back my chair and left the dining room. What a grouch Julia was! I bet she wouldn't tell me about any early rejections of her manuscripts because she'd had a million of them.

In the entry hall Aunt Thea met me with a smile. "I've got fresh orange juice and cinnamon rolls in the sunroom," she said. "You probably didn't feel like eating much breakfast, Samantha. Why don't you settle in with me, and we'll nibble on rolls and enjoy the storm?"

"You enjoy storms too?" I asked.

She put an arm around my shoulders, and I put one of mine around her waist. In spite of my anger at Augustus, I really wouldn't have walked out on Aunt Thea. I was glad that I had told Mrs. Engstrom I'd changed my mind about leaving.

When we'd settled into comfortable chairs in the sunroom, I asked Aunt Thea some of the same questions I'd asked Mrs. Engstrom. Aunt Thea was an intelligent, active woman, and I couldn't imagine that she'd be happy hidden away here, trying to placate her husband. As she talked about some of the famous people they'd visited and who had visited them in New York and here on the island, I tried to figure it out. She was here either because she was still very much in love with Augustus, or because she was afraid of him, or because . . . maybe . . .

I began to wonder if he might have some hold over her. He'd included Thea in the game. Did that mean she had a secret in her past life? One too awful to be made public?

But Thea was Augustus Trevor's wife! What kind of a monster would terrify his own wife?

Laura came into the room and sat on one of the wicker couches. She stretched out and sighed dramatically before she said, "Whatever Augustus plans to do, I wish he'd get it over with. This waiting is horrible. I tried to call my agent, and would you believe, because of the storm your phone is out."

Alex, still carrying his coffee cup, wandered in, stared out the windows for a moment, then perched next to Laura. "I hate rain," he said. "It makes everything look dreary."

"I'm sorry about the storm," Thea said. "I'm sure none of us slept well."

"As a matter of fact I did," Alex said. He drained the cup and put it on a nearby table. "I even slept quite late this morning."

"Probably because you were up so late last night," Laura said.

He shot her a glance from the corners of his eyes. "I wasn't up late. We all went upstairs together, as I remember."

Laura shook her head. "Your room is next to mine. I heard you moving around and your door opening and closing. I looked at my bedside clock, and it was nearly midnight."

I perked up and listened carefully. Had it been Alex at my door?

"I don't know what you heard, but it wasn't me," Alex insisted.

"It couldn't have been anyone else."

"Laura dear," he said, "you're beginning to sound like a busybody."

Laura apparently decided not to continue the argument, but she pressed her lips together in a pout and glared at Alex before she said, "You're such an inspiring person, Alex. It's wonderful how you managed to achieve so much when you had the terrible handicap of a dysfunctional childhood."

"Laura . . ." The word sounded like a warning.

"Even changing your name," she said. "Of course, I suppose that didn't bother you, since you never knew your parents and Alex Chambers has so much more . . . marketing appeal than—what was it? Keriomaglopolous or something like that?"

Thea reached over and patted Alex's arm. "No one's childhood is perfect," she said. "If you had a difficult time, then I'm sure it helped you to be even more sympathetic and understanding of others."

He glanced sharply, questioningly, at Thea, mumbled "Thank you," then stared down at his white ostrich boots as though he hadn't seen them before.

His air of conceit had vanished, and I felt sorry for him for thinking he needed it as a security blanket. Why couldn't he be proud that he'd been able to rise above his early poverty?

Julia wandered into the sun-room, complaining, "So here's where everyone is gathering. No one told me." She dragged a small wooden chair from its place by the wall, in order to sit close to the group. "Arthur's furious," she announced. "He tried to get through to his Washington office, but your phone isn't working."

"I'm sorry," Thea apologized. "We often lose phone service during bad weather."

Laura sighed. "When *is* this dreadful storm going to be over?"

Lucy, who had just arrived with fresh hot coffee, said, "Mrs. Trevor, the weather reporter on the radio said he's not counting on good weather until Monday or Tuesday."

There was a general groan, but Thea said, "Thank you, Lucy. If you see Senator Maggio, will you please ask him to join us?"

"Yes, ma'am," Lucy said, but as she left the room the senator and Buck passed her.

"We heard voices," Buck said, and he pulled up another of the small, straight-backed chairs that stood against the wall. Senator Maggio did the same, squeezing his chair into the circle. It occurred to me that we were like a group of pioneers, drawing our wagons into a ring for protection.

Buck was his unruly, beefy self, but Senator Maggio probably looked worse than anyone else in the room. His face sagged, and his eyes were sunken behind such dark circles, he looked as though someone had punched him.

"I'm afraid you didn't get much sleep last night," Thea said gently. "Didn't the hot milk help?"

"Not a bit," he said, then quickly added, "but you were kind to prepare it for me."

Thea smiled at him. "It's fortunate that we were both restless at the same time."

"So you were downstairs too," Laura said. She smiled and tossed a sharp glance in Alex's direction. "Thea, did you, by any chance, run into Alex? Around midnight?"

Thea shook her head. "It was after two when I decided I'd never get to sleep and I wandered down to the kitchen."

Now it was Alex's turn to stare smugly at Laura.

So . . . Senator Maggio had been wandering around the house last night too. But then, so had Aunt Thea. I still couldn't figure out who had been at my door.

Julia let out a long, aggrieved sigh. "That's neither here nor there," she said. "We're all waiting for Augustus to make his next move. Where is he?"

"He's usually down by this time," Thea said, and looked at her watch. She pressed a little button by her chair, and in less than a minute Walter appeared.

"Will you please see what's keeping Mr. Trevor?" she asked, and with a nod Walter left.

We could hear voices in the entry hall, and we all listened, thinking Walter had met up with Augustus, but one voice was a woman's, and it sounded sharp and agitated. It must have been Lucy's.

"You seem to have a devoted staff," Julia said. "I can't imagine how you'd find anyone willing to live out here away from civilization."

"I suppose we're very fortunate," Thea answered. "Lucy and Tomás, our cook, have been with us just a short while, and Walter only a year or two longer; but Frances Engstrom has been in our employ for over thirty years, and has become a dear and close friend."

"Only you, Thea, would make friends of the household

help," Julia said, and rolled her eyes, but I thought it was nice that Thea and Mrs. Engstrom were good friends.

The senator pointedly looked at his watch and grunted with exasperation, while Buck said, "Take it easy, Arthur. We aren't going anywhere."

"I'd like to get this so-called game over with," Senator Maggio said.

Alex began to answer him, but again we heard voices in the hall, and there was no mistaking that somebody was *very* upset.

We were all staring toward the open doorway when Mrs. Engstrom, Lucy, and Walter appeared. Mrs. Engstrom was pale and she fought to regain her balance as a tearful Lucy clung to her. "Mrs. Trevor," Mrs. Engstrom said, but her voice wobbled and she couldn't continue.

Walter made an effort to collect himself. He stood a little taller, took a deep breath, and said, "Mrs. Trevor, Lucy discovered that Mr. Trevor's bed had not been slept in, so I went to his office to see if he had spent the night there on the couch."

He gulped, and I could see his Adam's apple wobble up and down before he continued. "I'm sorry, Mrs. Trevor. Mr. Trevor is dead."

Thea gasped and half rose to her feet, but Lucy shrieked, "He's not just dead, Mrs. Trevor! There's blood on his head, and there's blood splattered on his desk! Mr. Trevor was murdered!"

SIX

Lucy had been right about the blood. There was a lot of it. We all rushed to the door of Augustus's office and tried to push and elbow our way inside—but not too far inside. It was as though we really couldn't believe what had happened to Augustus unless we actually saw it for ourselves.

Augustus Trevor was seated in his chair, his head on the desk next to the computer keyboard. One bent arm covered his face.

This was not a TV cop show in which the problem would be over in half an hour. Augustus Trevor had been a real person whose life had been taken away. I suddenly felt sick. For a moment it was hard to breathe, and I found that I was shaking. I held on to the door frame for support and took a couple of long, shuddering breaths to steady myself. The horrible feeling gradually slid away, and I knew I'd be able to handle the situation.

However, Laura moaned softly and gracefully sank to the floor, sitting with her back against the wall, her hands clasped in her lap while silent tears spilled from her closed eyelids. I would have offered to help her—at least bring her a glass of water—except that I'd seen her do exactly the same thing when she was playing the part of a woman whose husband went off to battle in that Revolutionary War movie she starred in a few years ago.

Alex gagged, turned white, and ran from the room, shoving Buck aside with more strength than I'd thought he had.

"Ouch!" Buck muttered as he staggered into the pointed open drawer of a nearby file cabinet.

I suddenly remembered Thea and turned to look for her. She was standing just outside the door, Mrs. Engstrom's arms around her.

"She'll be all right," Mrs. Engstrom said as her glance met mine. "It's a terrible shock, but don't worry. She'll be all right."

I nodded. Thea's face hadn't lost its color, and she seemed to be in good hands.

I went back to the door of the office as Senator Maggio ordered everyone, "Stay away from the crime scene. There's evidence here that should be protected."

"If you're looking for the murder weapon, it's probably that fireplace thing," Julia said, and pointed at the sharp-ended brass poker that lay on the floor.

There were dark stains near the point, so she might have been right; but something else had caught my attention. The mesh screen across the fireplace that would normally have been closed was open, and lying among the ashes were some curled and cracked metal and plastic pieces.

"Look at the fireplace," I told the others. "Someone has burned some computer disks."

In one bound Buck fell to his knees before the fireplace and groped among the ashes, jerking out the disks and making a terrible mess. "There's scraps of paper too," Buck said. "Looks like typing paper."

He got to his feet, one hand holding aloft the disks and a couple of scorched corners from typing paper—one with the page number 395 printed on it—while he tried to wipe the ashes from his other hand on the seat of his jeans.

"Do you think those are the backup disks containing the manuscript Augustus was telling us about?" Julia asked.

"I hope so," Laura answered, and I saw that she was back on her feet.

"Turn on the computer," Julia said. "There must be a file. . . ."

Senator Maggio flipped the Off switch and said, "I've already tried it. There's no file. Everything has been wiped out."

"If someone destroyed the file, the manuscript, and the disks, he's put an end to the threat," Alex said from behind me. Apparently he'd made a quick recovery.

Julia's mouth twisted as she added, "And put an end to Augustus, as well."

"Who did it?" Laura whispered.

A long moment of silence followed as we all realized that one person in this room was a murderer. I could feel tickly drops of sweat skitter down my backbone, and I shivered. "The murderer has to be someone who's familiar with computers," I said, "someone who'd know how to delete the file."

Julia was the first to respond. "I don't use a computer. I write in longhand, and Jake types up the finished manuscript for me."

"I don't use a computer," the senator said.

"Me either," Buck answered.

Alex shook his head.

"Well, don't everybody look at me, for goodness' sakes," Laura complained. "I've never had a reason even to touch one of those things."

I didn't look at her. I glanced from Julia to Alex to Senator Maggio. No matter what they'd just said, a few minutes ago each of them had proved that they knew enough about computers to understand files and disks. Each of them was lying.

"We must notify the police," Senator Maggio said.

"We can't," I told him. "The phone lines are out. Remember?"

This called for another moment of silence. Each of us sneaked appraising looks at the others while trying not to be seen doing it.

Finally, Julia said, "Let's face some plain facts and look at the positive side. Whatever Augustus had in mind for us is over now."

I heard Thea's sharp intake of breath, and I wasn't the only one who was disgusted with Julia for being so insensitive. Senator Maggio scowled at her and asked in a low voice, "Are you forgetting that Trevor's wife is present?"

Julia looked embarrassed, but she said, "All I meant was that the manuscript has been destroyed."

"No, it hasn't," I said.

Everyone turned to look at me. "Everything on the hard disk in the computer was deleted, and the backup disks were burned, along with what looks like a printed copy of the manuscript," I told them, "but Aug-Augustus was a professional writer. He wouldn't print just one copy of his manuscript. He'd have made one to send to his agent—which he said hadn't been sent yet—and one for himself. Even though the manuscript would be on his computer's hard disk and on backup disks, writers always make at least two printed copies of everything they write."

"How do you know all this?" Laura asked me.

"I read the writers' magazines." I turned to Julia for support. "You're a writer. You do the same thing with your manuscripts, don't you?"

Julia's mouth opened and closed and opened again. "Well, sure," she said. "My—um—secretary does."

Mrs. Engstrom asked Aunt Thea, "Is it true what your niece said?"

"Yes," Thea answered. "Augustus always made a second copy of every completed manuscript."

"Where did he keep the copies?" the senator asked.

"He always kept his notes and materials for whatever manuscript he was working on currently in the top drawer of that file cabinet." She pointed, and we all turned to look. It was the drawer that had been standing open. "Since he said the manuscript had been completed, there should have been two copies of the manuscript in that drawer, as well."

Buck peered inside and shook his head. "It's empty."

"Maybe both copies were burned." Laura's voice was high-pitched and excited with hope.

The senator bent to study the contents of the fireplace. "I doubt it," he said. "Considering that we know there were at least three hundred and ninety-five typewritten pages in that manuscript, if not more, there isn't enough ash here to account for two manuscripts."

"If there's another copy, then we should look for it," Alex said.

"Do we really want it found?" Laura asked.

"I think we do," the senator answered. "It will show up sooner or later, and if it got into the wrong hands, it might pose a future threat."

"Are you talking about blackmail?" Buck asked.

No one needed to give the obvious answer, so Julia said, "We'll find the manuscript, then destroy it without reading it. Agreed?"

"Agreed," everyone said.

I was glad that none of them asked *me* to agree, because the real reason for finding the manuscript, as far as I was concerned, would be to read it in order to discover which of the guests had a reason for murdering Augustus.

Buck said, "If Augustus hid it, then it's probably somewhere in this room."

"We could divide the room into sections," Julia suggested. "Two of us could take the bookcase, two the file cabinets, one the desk . . ."

"Ohhh," Laura murmured. "While . . . uh . . . Augustus is still here?"

I couldn't stand it any longer and shouted, "You can't decide to search this room! It isn't your house! It's Aunt Thea's house!"

Thea moved closer and took my hand. Even though I was upset, I noticed that Mrs. Engstrom moved too, positioning herself in such a way that she blocked Augustus's body from Thea's view. She *was* a good friend. I knew that in the same situation, I would have done anything to help Darlene, and she would have done the same for me.

"Samantha dear," Thea said, "what happened to Augustus is horrible beyond belief." Her fingers trembled, and I could feel shivers vibrate throughout her body. "But I've been heartsick at this terrible game—as Augustus called it. I can't believe that he could have threatened and frightened our guests as he did. It was unforgivable of him. I agree with them that the manuscript should be found."

"Before the police get here?"

There was a slight, silent pause, as though everyone in the room had stopped breathing until Aunt Thea said, "I think, under the circumstances, that finding the manuscript *before* the police arrive would be preferable."

That was laying it on the line. I reminded myself that Aunt Thea was one of the game-players, too, and she'd want that manuscript found and all evidence of *her* secret destroyed. I didn't think that finding and destroying the manuscript was such a good idea, but it wasn't my house, my secret past, or my husband who'd been murdered. About the only thing I could do would be to stay out of the way.

"Let's get busy," Julia said.

Senator Maggio took charge by immediately making up a list of rules and assigning everyone places. They went to their particular sections and began removing books, papers, anything in sight—only neatly, putting them back the way they had been, so everything would be in order when the police arrived.

As I watched them work—no one had thought about giving me a job—I had a chance to go over things that had been said, and I began to wonder about Julia. She was a writer. She should know about the importance of manuscript copies. Yet she was the first one to tell us that the manuscript had been destroyed. And at breakfast she hadn't remembered her own stories and characters. I knew, from reading what writers had to say about writing, that after living with her characters for months— maybe even years while she was plotting and writing about them—they'd be like real people. How could she forget them?

Buck had worked gingerly through each side of the desk, opening drawers with a handkerchief, and taking care not to touch Augustus; but he'd finished, finding nothing, and had joined Julia, who was meticulously removing books from the large bookcase and peering behind them.

I had seen something protruding from under the sleeve of Augustus's velvet jacket, near his right elbow. It seemed to be a small stack of envelopes, and they looked very much like those that held the clues Augustus had given to his guests the night before. I quietly walked over and slid out the stack, turned them over, and on the top, printed in bright blue ink, was the name *Alex Chambers, Game Clue #2.*

I thumbed through the envelopes and, just as I thought, there was one for each of the guests and one for Aunt Thea. Augustus had told them he'd have more clues for them to figure out. Obviously, here was the batch he probably had intended to hand out right after breakfast.

Buck leaned against the bookcase, his face more flushed than ever. "That manuscript is not in this room," he said. "Are we going to have to search the entire house?"

"We don't have a choice," the senator told him.

But I held up the envelopes and said, "Yes, you do. These must be the next set of clues."

"Clues for what?" Laura asked. "Weren't they for finding some kind of a treasure?"

I shrugged. "I think the manuscript was supposed to be the treasure."

They all just stared at me, no one saying anything, so I explained. "He said it would be a significant treasure. Okay, what's significant about the treasure hunt? Remember, he said that if you could solve the clues you could get your story removed from his manuscript? It makes sense, then, doesn't it, that the clue solvers would find the manuscript itself?"

"It does make sense," the senator said slowly, "especially since it seems as though the manuscript has been hidden."

"So you might find it through the clues," I said, and again held up the envelopes.

"It's worth a try," Julia said. She stepped up and pulled the envelopes from my hand, riffling through them until she found the one with her name on it.

She shoved the other envelopes back in my hand and started out of the room, but I called out, "Wait a minute. It could take forever if you work alone. Why don't you try to solve the clues together?"

"I don't think so," Senator Maggio said, "not if they're like the first set Augustus gave us."

Thea said, "I'm going to be blunt about it. If your clues were like mine, then they let you know exactly what it was Augustus planned to include about each of you in his book."

"You're right!" Laura said, and groaned. "No one's going to see my clue."

"What if no one understood the clue except you?" I asked. "And what if you put all the clues together and came up with where the manuscript is hidden?"

"I don't know," Buck said, and rubbed so hard at his chin as he thought about it, I was afraid the skin would come off.

"I don't like the idea of sharing information," Julia announced.

"Okay," I said. "It was just an idea. For that matter, you have all weekend to go through every chest and trunk and cupboard and closet in this whole huge house. You might find the manuscript that way."

For a moment they were silent, and I knew they were thinking of all the rooms in this house—each one packed with furniture which could hold a manuscript. The hunt could still be on by the time the storm was over and the police arrived.

"I like Samantha's idea," Alex said, surprising me. "But I want to put a qualifier in there. I suggest we take a short break and read our clues. If they're not as personal as our first set of clues, then it does make sense to share them. We can meet in the dining room in about half an hour."

Laura hesitated. "What should we do about those first clues Augustus gave us?"

"Let's just see what's in this second set before we decide anything," he answered.

Laura glanced at me. "If we're going to try to figure this out together, could Sam help? She showed us how fast she was at figuring out her own clue."

I kept quiet. Now was no time for explanations. Besides, I wanted to be in on the hunt.

"I think Samantha would be an asset to us," Thea answered.

Senator Maggio smoothed down a single strand of hair over his bald head and grimaced. "I suppose we're all in this together. All right. I have no objections."

"Then let's get out of here and get to work," Julia said.

They quickly filed from the room, but I hesitated, picking up a legal-sized, lined note pad and a pen from one side of the desk.

Thea was the last to leave, and I waited for her until she'd quietly closed the office door. She paused only to glance toward the desk. There was no shock in her expression, just an agonizing mix of pain and hurt and sorrow that lasted only a few seconds.

"I deeply regret that you had to see him like this," Mrs. Engstrom said. She took Aunt Thea's arm and ushered her down the hallway and toward the stairs.

I tagged along behind them, walking a lot more slowly than I would have liked. I couldn't wait to see those clues!

SEVEN

One half hour later we seated ourselves around the highly polished table and waited. Julia cleared her throat a few times, Laura sniffled, and Buck made a kind of humming growl that vibrated around his tonsils. We were like members of an orchestra waiting for a conductor to raise his baton as a signal that we should begin.

The senator must have decided to take the lead, because he said, "I assume that we have all read our clues. I, for one, have determined that mine is not personal in nature, as the first clue was."

He removed the sheet of paper inside the envelope in his hand and laid it directly in front of him on the table.

The others—Thea and Laura hesitating more than the rest—finally followed his example.

I had sat next to Laura on purpose, and I brazenly leaned over her shoulder in order to read what was typed on her sheet of paper. Right in the middle of this blank white space were the words ONE WILL BE ABOVE ALL: THE TEN OF SPADES'.

Laura turned so that our noses were almost touching. "Okay, tell," she whispered. "What does it mean?"

"I don't know . . . yet," I said, reluctant to give up my super-sleuth reputation. "We need to see the others."

No one else had spoken. The senator scowled at his paper as though, if he intimidated it enough, it would speak. Buck squinted hard at his clue and rubbed his chin again, while Alex and Julia glanced up from their papers to study the other faces in the room.

"Have any of you figured your clues out yet?" Julia asked. "Mine tells me nothing."

"What does it say?" Laura asked.

Julia held her paper a little closer to her chest and turned toward the senator. "Have we decided if we're going to share them?"

"Oh, for goodness' sakes," Laura said. She slapped her paper out flat on the table where anyone could see it and read it aloud. "Mine is nothing but the name of a dumb playing card. Did we all get the same thing?"

"Not exactly," Alex answered. "Mine begins in the same way: ONE WILL BE ABOVE ALL. But I've got the king of diamonds."

"Jack of clubs," Buck said, and tossed his paper into the center of the table.

"I have the nine of diamonds," Thea said.

"All right," Julia added, and laid her sheet of paper in front of her. "Mine is the queen of hearts."

There was a pause before Senator Maggio intoned, as though he'd just been picked king of the hill, "If this were a card game, I'd beat you all. Mine is the ace of spades, highest in point value."

"Not always," I told him. "In cribbage an ace is at the bottom and only worth one point."

I realized, by the look on his face, that I wasn't exactly his favorite person, so I tried to get back to the subject of the clues. "Does each of your clues begin the same way, with the words ONE WILL BE ABOVE ALL?"

They nodded, and the senator said, "I was trying to make the point that the ace is above all other cards."

"Except . . ." I began, then changed my mind. There was a more important point to make. "Laura's is possessive."

"That's not true," Laura said. "I am not."

"Not you," I said, "your ten of spades. See . . . there's an apostrophe after it. Do the rest of them have an apostrophe?"

"They all do," Julia said. "What does that mean?"

"One more thing for us to figure out," I answered.

Thea interrupted. "Samantha was right in suggesting we work together. Apparently that's what Augustus intended us to do." She sighed and added, "He set us apart with the first clues, then probably intended to see how long it would take us to realize we had to work together on the second."

Julia shrugged and said, "Okay, Sam, since you know so much about it, what are we supposed to do now with these stupid clues?"

"Well," I said, a little nervous because everyone was staring at me as though I had the answer written on my forehead, "we should look for other meanings to the clues and try as many angles as we can."

"Like what?" Laura asked.

"You've got a spade," I said. "What else does a spade mean?"

Her eyes began to glimmer all green and golden as the thought struck her. "Oh!" she said, "a spade! Does that mean we're supposed to dig for something?" She made a face. "In this rainstorm? How could Augustus do that to us?"

"He didn't know it was going to rain," I said, "and we don't know if that's what it means." I looked across the table at Julia. "What about your queen of hearts?"

She tried to look modest and didn't make it. "Perhaps it refers to me as the reigning queen of romantic novels."

Laura's lip curled. "I'd hardly call your stories *romantic*, dear."

Julia had her mouth open to respond, but Thea suddenly began to chant, " 'The Queen of Hearts, she baked some tarts, all on a summer's day.' Could the clue lead to the kitchen? The Queen of Hearts' tarts?"

"Maybe," I answered. I was writing everything down as fast as I could.

"What about a real heart?" Buck asked. "Augustus didn't have one pickled in a bottle or anything like that, did he?"

"Of course not," Thea said, and shuddered.

"I wish he'd had a *change* of heart," Alex muttered.

I ignored them as I looked up at Aunt Thea and said, "You had the nine of diamonds. Does that mean anything special? Like, do you have nine diamonds?"

"More than nine," she answered, "but would the clue have to refer to real diamonds? I've been thinking about the diamond pattern of the tiles in the hallway."

"There's baseball diamonds," Buck added.

"Crystalline carbon," Senator Maggio said.

"What?"

"The chemical composition of a diamond."

I doubted that Augustus had thought in that direction, but I wrote down what the senator had to say, as well.

"Anyone else with a diamond?" I asked.

"I have the king of diamonds," Alex answered.

"King," I said, "monarch, pharaoh, ruler . . ."

"Aha!" said the senator. "Ruler . . . a tool with which we measure. I think we may be on to something here."

Buck shook his head. "I've got the jack of clubs. So what do you make of that? A club is a weapon."

"It may also be something social," the senator answered.

"Oh, yeah," Buck said. "Like a softball club, or the Lions Club, or the Rotary Club." A pleased kind of grin warmed his face. "I just got an award from the Rotary Club in Wickasee, Ohio, for being an outstanding role model to kids."

"That's lovely, Buck," Thea said.

But Julia snapped, "Come on, come on. It's no big deal. We all get awards. What we've got to work on now are these clues."

Laura poked me in the ribs and whispered, "Well? Well?"

"Give me time," I mumbled, and said to the group, "I think we have to keep in mind the words that begin all the clues: ONE WILL BE ABOVE ALL. From what we've learned so far, what do you think this means?"

"If we're talking about the cards themselves," Alex said, "spades are the top suit."

"Suit, maybe," Senator Maggio said, looking firmly at me, "but in card value we're back to the ace."

"Or it could be the king," I insisted.

Alex spoke up. "Has anyone noticed there's a run of ace, king, queen, jack, ten, and nine? Could that mean anything?"

No one answered. In case it did, I quickly wrote down the clues in order along with the initials of the people who held the card clues, hoping this might spell out something. The first part was zilch, and the last three initials spelt out BLT, which made me realize I was awfully hungry and would give anything right now for a bacon, lettuce, and tomato sandwich on white toast. It seemed kind of disrespectful to think of lunch when we were trying to find a missing manuscript and I was trying to discover the identity of a murderer, but I couldn't help it.

Once again I looked at what I had copied under the heading *Game Clues* #2:

ONE WILL BE ABOVE ALL:	THE ACE OF SPADES'	M.
"	THE KING OF DIAMONDS'	A.
"	THE QUEEN OF HEARTS'	J.
"	THE JACK OF CLUBS'	B.
"	THE TEN OF SPADES'	L.
"	THE NINE OF DIAMONDS'	T.

Finally, Julia said, "Let's think in a different direction. If Augustus meant *things*, not *cards*, then in value you can't beat diamonds."

"Good point," I said. I made some more notes.

Mrs. Engstrom appeared at the door. "Are you finished, Mrs. Trevor?" she asked, and her next words warmed my heart. "Lucy would like to set the table for lunch."

"Thank you, Mrs. Engstrom. We haven't finished, but we can take our work to the sun-room," Thea answered.

The senator pushed back his chair. "I don't think we're going to finish, unless we have more to go on than this."

"We could share the first clues," I suggested.

I was surprised when Thea said, "No! I don't think we need to do that. At least not yet."

Buck got up. "What about your clue, Sam? That special clue Augustus gave you. Didn't he say something about it making more sense than the rest of them?"

"He was kidding, because it didn't," I mumbled.

"Didn't it?"

They all stared at me again, but I didn't feel like telling them the rude message Augustus had given me, so I quickly asked them all, "May I keep these clues for a little while? I'd like to study them and see if there isn't something—maybe even in the typing of them—that we're missing."

When no one objected, Buck shrugged and Julia nodded. They left the room with the senator and Alex, allowing me to gather the sheets of paper. Aunt Thea graciously put her clue into my hand and smiled at me, while Laura shoved hers at me and said, "You've got to solve this quickly, Sam. We haven't much time."

She and Thea walked from the room. I hurried to pick up all the sheets of paper and catch up with them, but Mrs. Engstrom put a hand on my arm, detaining me.

"Miss Burns," she said softly, "I hope you'll be able to help your aunt."

"I do too," I said.

"I'm glad that after you find the manuscript, it will be destroyed before anyone has read it."

I liked the confidence she had in me. She didn't say *if* I found it. It was *when* I found it, but she was still looking at me with a pleading, hopeful look in her eyes, so I said, "Mrs. Engstrom, I don't agree. The contents of the manuscript might help us discover who the murderer is."

"If the things he wrote about were made known," she said, twisting the word *he* as though it tasted bitter in her mouth, "they could destroy innocent people."

"Things" had to refer to Thea. I doubted if Mrs. Engstrom cared that much about the others or thought any of them to be innocent. She and I both knew that one of them was a murderer.

Her steady gaze made me so uncomfortable, I quickly said, "Believe me, I wouldn't hurt Aunt Thea for anything," and hurried out of the room.

I didn't join the others in the sun-room. I took my pad and pen and the clues to my room, then walked down the hall to Augustus Trevor's bedroom. I needed more answers, and I hoped I could find them there.

A key, almost exactly like mine, protruded from the keyhole in his bedroom door. The door was locked, so I held my breath while I turned the key and slowly opened the door. The room was so silent and dark, I quickly fumbled for the light switch before I closed the door behind me. It was cold, too, and I felt clammy, as though dampness from the storm had seeped through the walls. I saw that the heating vents had been closed and wondered why anyone would want to sleep in this depressing, cavelike room.

I didn't care for Augustus Trevor's tastes. Over the windows heavy, tapestry-like draperies had been drawn, shutting out most of the light. The massive high-posted, king-size bed was covered with a spread made of the same dull tapestry; and a maroon overstuffed chair, brass lamp, and table were grouped in one corner of the room. The table, chest of drawers, and wardrobe were of dark, carved mahogany, and all sorts of framed photographs of famous people cluttered not only the walls of the room, but also the tops of the chest and the table.

Mixed among the standing photographs were a lot of carvings of animals and fish. I supposed they were very expensive and valuable, but if this had been *my* bedroom, I'd have tossed them out and put up posters instead. Who wants to see, first thing in the morning, a hideous green jade frog with his tongue lolling out. Yuck!

When I cautiously opened the top drawer in the chest of drawers, I could see that the contents had been pawed through. Everything inside the drawer was a mess, and I was positive that wasn't the way Walter kept Augustus's things. Someone had been looking for the missing manuscript and thought, as I had, that Augustus would have kept it close by—if not in his office, then in his bedroom.

Had whoever it was found it?

As I opened the rest of the drawers and looked into them, I was pretty sure that the manuscript had not been found, because the contents of every single one of the drawers had been stirred through.

I found myself standing next to another door, and this one had a key in it as well. I turned the knob, but the door was locked. It had to be the door to a bathroom, but why lock it? I asked myself, and I immediately began to wonder if the person who had searched this room had checked out the bathroom as well. Bathrooms had closets or cabinets. What if Augustus had wrapped his manuscript in towels or sheets, thinking no one would ever think of looking in a bathroom?

Well, I would!

I unlocked the door and opened it to find a large white-and-black-tiled bathroom that was even colder than the bedroom, if possible. Rain beat at the small window, seeping through the crack at the bottom and staining the wall like tear streaks down a dirty face. A white shower curtain closed off the tub, and I ignored it, trying not to think of that scary *Psycho* movie Mom and Dad had rented in which a woman gets stabbed in a shower. I took baths, instead of showers, for months after I saw that movie.

I opened the built-in cabinet that reached from floor to ceiling, and was pleased to see that the sheets and towels and all the other stuff people keep in bathrooms—like extra boxes of tissue and hot-water bottles—hadn't been disturbed.

So I disturbed them. I was neater than the person who'd searched the bedroom had been. I took out stacks of things, looked through, around, and behind them, then put them back the way they'd been. It was hard because I had to work fast, and—unfortunately—it was all for nothing. The manuscript hadn't been hidden in the bathroom.

All that bending and stretching had made me tired. I shoved the shower curtain aside so that I could sit on the edge of the tub, but instead I froze in midair.

I clung to the curtain with fingers as tight and stiff as claws, unable to move. My mouth was open, but not a sound came out, and—as though I were a bird trapped by a snake—I couldn't look away. Augustus Trevor's bloody, twisted face stared up at me from the bottom of the tub!

EIGHT

"What are you doing in here?" a low voice asked.

That did it. The words broke the spell, terrifying me so much, I nearly fell on top of Augustus. Grabbing the shower curtain for support, I swung around and out and slammed into Walter, who clutched my shoulders and kept me on my feet.

"Downstairs . . . in his office . . . bathtub . . . two of him? No, couldn't be . . . but where . . . why?"

"Be quiet please, Miss Burns," Walter said. "If you'll stop making so much noise, I'll explain." He gave me a gentle push in the direction of the bedroom and pulled the shower curtain closed before he followed me out of the bathroom and locked the door again. This time he pocketed the key.

"Since it will be at least a day or two before the storm will subside and we'll be able to notify the police, I deemed it prudent to—um—store Mr. Trevor's body in a room which could be kept at a cool temperature."

"Oh," I said. "But what about when the police get here? Won't they mind? Doesn't the body have to be just the way it was when we found it? I mean, maybe they'd see clues that would tell who murdered him, although—"

"You didn't answer my question," Walter interrupted, and his tone of voice was less like a butler and more like our suspicious next-door neighbor when she used to ask, "Who threw the ball into my petunia bed? Was it you, Samantha?"

I wanted to be straightforward about everything with Walter, so I told him that I couldn't decipher the second group of clues we'd been given, and I hoped that if I looked around Augustus's bedroom I'd learn something that would help.

"And find the manuscript?" he asked.

"Well, I guess I had that in mind too."

"Did you find it?"

"All I discovered was that someone else searched the room before I did," I answered, and explained about the messy drawers. "Whoever it was must have been looking for the manuscript."

"Do you think they found it?"

"No," I said. "I'm pretty sure they didn't."

Walter rose an inch taller and became a butler again. "Luncheon has been served," he said. "I was sent to find you."

Lunch? I'd forgotten all about it, but my stomach hadn't, because it began to growl.

When I entered the dining room, everyone stopped talking and looked at me. I was getting awfully tired of being the center of attention.

"Well?" Laura asked. "Well?"

"I haven't had enough time!" I happened to glance at myself in the mirror over the sideboard and saw that my face showed my irritation, so I tried to calm down.

No sooner was I seated, with my napkin in my lap and a salad—with more of those strange, crunchy things—in front of me, than Senator Maggio nodded in my direction, peered from under his thick eyebrows, and asked, "Where have you been?"

"In Augustus Trevor's bedroom," I said.

"Why, dear?" Aunt Thea's eyes widened in surprise.

"There are two places most people would hide things in, because they're personal places," I said. "So I figured that Augustus would hide whatever he wanted to hide either in his office or in his bedroom. I thought I'd look."

"Aren't you the one who said we should work on clues instead of wasting time searching for the manuscript?" Julia demanded.

"Well, yes," I said, "but we can't get very far with just one set of clues." I took a large bite of salad. It tasted good, but what *was* that curly purple stuff?

"Wait a minute," she said. "You were looking for *clues*?"

"Both."

The senator put down his fork, his salad untasted. "Augustus spoke of giving us clues throughout the weekend. There must be a series of clues he'd prepared for us. The question is, where are they?"

"What did you find, Samantha?" Thea asked.

"No clues and no manuscript," I said, "but I did find that someone had already searched through all the drawers in the chest and the wardrobe."

No one spoke up. I guess it was dumb to expect someone to say "I did it." Everyone at the table shot questioning glances at the others, though, and everyone except Buck just poked at their salads. Buck ate every bite of his. Oh, well, for that matter, I did too.

Finally, Senator Maggio said, "We have to assume that one of us found the manuscript and is in possession of it."

"No, we don't," I said. There I was, contradicting him again, and it was obvious by the thundercloud expression on his face that he didn't like it.

"What I mean is," I continued, trying to make the situation less tense, "all the drawers were a mess. If the manuscript had been found at some point in the search, then we could even tell where it had been, because some of the drawers wouldn't have been touched. The prowler wouldn't have needed to keep looking."

"Good point," Julia said.

The senator didn't give in graciously. "Perhaps one of us—or all of us—should look carefully through the room to make sure that Samantha was correct in what she found."

"Oh, really," Thea began, but I just shrugged.

"It's fine with me," I answered, "only don't go in the bathroom."

"Why not?" Buck asked.

"Because Augustus Trevor is in the bathtub."

"What?" Julia shouted, and Laura screeched.

"Please, everyone, don't get upset," Aunt Thea quickly said, and she went on to explain why Walter had moved the body—after consulting her, of course.

"I can understand your reasoning," Senator Maggio said, "but the police may not accept it. Evidence leading to the identity of the murderer may have been destroyed."

"Oh, don't be so pompous, Arthur!" Julia snapped. "What's done is done, and for that matter, do any of us care who murdered Augustus? I don't!"

"Me either," Laura said.

I couldn't stand it. Everything that had happened around here was making me crazy. "Please don't talk like that. He was Aunt Thea's husband," I reminded them. "Besides, if you just think about it, whoever murdered him could murder you too."

Laura gasped, but Alex said quietly, "The only one who would need to worry is the person who might accidentally discover the murderer's identity."

"Please!" Aunt Thea held out her hands almost as though she were begging, then dropped them into her lap.

Senator Maggio looked sternly in my direction. "We must respect each other's privacy, Samantha," he said. "I'd like to know why you gave yourself permission to open a locked door."

Walter came in and began removing the salad plates and substituting some kind of soup with chunks of tomatoes and shrimp in it. His expression was unreadable, and he didn't look in my direction.

It didn't matter. I had something to ask the senator. "How did you know that the door was locked?"

For a moment Senator Maggio's eyes widened, and he made a flapping fish mouth while he tried to think of what to say next. But he quickly recovered and answered smoothly, "I passed the door as I was coming downstairs and saw the key in the lock. Just to make sure that the room was secured, I checked the knob and was gratified to discover that the door was locked."

"Did you know that the bathroom door was locked?"

"Of course not," he said. "I'd have no way of knowing that."

I couldn't tell if he was lying or not. I thought he was.

"I can't take much more of this," Alex blurted out. "While we're eating lunch, I don't want to hear another word about the murder! We have to talk about something —anything—else."

There was silence for a moment. Then Buck said, "What d'ya think of the Green Bay Packers' chances this year?"

"Chances for what?" Laura asked.

Buck made kind of a choking sound.

Julia said, "My agent called on Tuesday. *Starved for Love* is going into video."

No one said anything. The only sound in the room was Buck slurping his soup.

"I'm due back in Washington on Friday for those confirmation hearings on Martinez," Senator Maggio told us. "They should be routine. I'm sure she'll get Senate approval."

No one wanted to add to that, so again there was a long, miserable silence. The dining room was an interior room and didn't have windows, but the storm was still loud enough that I could hear bursts of rain and wind slamming against the house.

"After the studio paired me with that overaged bozo on my last film," Laura suddenly said, "I demanded casting approval on the next." She looked at all the uninterested faces and added, her voice gradually fading away, "There isn't exactly a contract yet, but we're working things out, you understand."

Maybe no one understood, because no one answered.

Finally, I laid my soup spoon on my plate, clutched the

edge of the table so hard, my fingers hurt, and said, "One set of clues isn't enough. If you'll share your first set of clues with me, I might be able to help you make some sense of all this."

"Those messages Augustus gave us won't help," Julia answered. "I don't think he meant them as clues. They each contained information that would prove to us that Augustus knew something about us we'd rather no one else knew."

Walter came in to take away the soup plates and bring in chocolate eclairs.

"None for me, thank you," Laura and Julia said together, but Buck reached out and clamped his fingers around Walter's wrist.

"I'll eat theirs," he said. For a moment I felt sorry for him. He was a big guy, and soup and salad probably weren't enough to fill him up.

When we had finished lunch and were waiting for Thea to stand, Alex suddenly said, "Augustus had planned to give us more clues."

"We know that," Julia grumbled.

Alex half stood as he reached into the hip pocket on his very snug jeans. He pulled out a wad of envelopes and laid them on the table. We all stared.

"What are those?" Senator Maggio asked, although we could see the names printed in blue ink and *Game Clue* #3 on them.

"Where did you get these?" Thea asked.

"Where'd these come from? What's this all about?" Buck asked.

"I happened upon them," Alex said.

"Where? When?"

For a moment Alex scowled. "Where and when doesn't matter. The point is, I found them."

In Augustus Trevor's bedroom? I thought. _It had to be. He had the second set of clues with him when he was murdered. Maybe he wanted to keep the third set in a private place until he was ready to give them out._

Julia stretched to reach the envelope with her name on it and slid it across the table until she could pick it up. "My envelope's been opened!" she complained.

"What difference does it make?" Alex asked.

"You opened all of them so you could read ours as well as yours!"

"That's right," he said. "I thought it would help me find the manuscript."

Senator Maggio put on his most forceful voice. "I assumed we were working together."

Alex just shrugged.

"Working together seems to be our only chance to succeed," Thea told him.

"You can see, from those playing card clues, that Augustus meant us to share ideas," Julia said.

Alex's voice was sharp as he turned toward her. "Only to a point. Remember, he also said that only those of us smart enough to figure out the clues would win."

Julia pushed back her chair, and her eyes narrowed with anger. "You're saying that Augustus expected some of us to cheat the others? The way you tried to cheat us by finding the clues and hiding them from us?"

"Maybe," Alex said. "In any case, I wasn't able to figure them out. Does that make you happy?"

"Deliriously," Julia snapped.

Laura sniffed self-righteously and said, "At least we know we can't trust Alex any longer."

"No sermons," Alex said. "I've given you the next set of clues. Do you want them, or not?"

Thea rose. "Let's take them to the sun-room."

I ran upstairs to get my pad and pen.

The little door at the head of the winding stairs to my tower room was standing ajar, although I knew I had locked it. I automatically reached for the key I'd shoved into my pocket and pulled it out, along with the folded paper with my GET LOST message on it.

I shoved them both back into my pocket and moved forward cautiously, peering around the edge of the door. The room was empty, but it was obvious that someone had searched it. The drawers of the small chest were open, the few things I'd brought had spilled out, and my jacket was lying on the floor, the pockets turned inside out.

Why would someone do this to *me*? I didn't have anything anyone would want.

Or did I?

Buck had talked about the clue Augustus had given me, repeating what Augustus had said. I'd tried to tell them all that it wasn't true my clue made more sense than theirs, that Augustus had only been joking; but it was plain, from the looks of my room, that at least one of them hadn't believed me. I wished now I hadn't been too embarrassed to tell them that the message had only been GET LOST.

I dumped my things back into the drawers and closed them; picked up the set of clues, pen, and pad, which were scattered across the bed; and left the room, carefully locking the door behind me.

There was something I had to find out. I walked down the long, empty hall, chose a door at random, and tried my key in the lock. It easily opened the door. Rats! As far as protection went, my key was good for nothing. All the bedroom door keys were probably made from the same mold.

I couldn't help glancing into the room. From the tie draped over the back of a chair, I knew it must be Senator Maggio's room. A dresser stood near the door, and I saw on top of it, next to a lap-top computer, the envelope Augustus had given the senator.

Whatever is in that envelope is none of my business, I told myself.

But I answered, *We're dealing with a murder. I need to find out as much as I can about the clues so I can help solve them, don't I?*

Do you want to be as sneaky as Alex?

It's not the same thing, I insisted. *If I solve the clues, it might keep someone else from being murdered.*

I didn't like arguing with myself, so I stepped inside the room, quickly opened the envelope, and found myself looking at a train schedule for a lot of small towns. I had no idea where. One name was circled: Bonino. It sounded familiar, but I had no idea where the town of Bonino was or what it meant as far as being a clue.

I returned the letter to the envelope, put it where it had been, and left the room. I had tucked the key into my pocket and was passing the door of the Red Room when it suddenly opened, and Lucy walked out. She was carrying a dusting cloth and a can of spray stuff in one hand, a small wastepaper basket in the other.

Lucy started when she saw me, but I smiled with relief

that I hadn't been caught in the senator's room. There was a question that had been bothering me, and Lucy could probably answer it.

"The door keys for the upstairs bedrooms are all for show, aren't they?" I asked. "I mean the same key fits every door."

"That's right," Lucy said.

"Isn't that a problem?"

She looked surprised. "Why should it be? The only people who come here are Mr. and Mrs. Trevor's guests. You don't have to lock doors against guests."

Even guests who sneak around in the middle of the night? I didn't want to tell Lucy about my midnight visitor, so I just nodded and said, "So none of the rooms can really be locked."

"Just the wine cellar," she said. "Mr. Trevor kept it locked, and that was a big nuisance for Walter and Tomás, especially when they needed to get wine during the times that Mr. Trevor couldn't be disturbed." She smiled. "Mr. Trevor was silly about that wine cellar. None of us were going to help ourselves to his wine."

A gust of wind rattled around the house, and Lucy shivered. "I wish the storm was over," she said. "I wish the phone company could fix the lines."

"So Aunt Thea could call the police," I added.

Lucy took a step closer to me and said, barely above a whisper, "I'm scared here. Aren't you?"

"Yes," I said.

"It's bad enough Mr. Trevor got himself murdered. I keep thinking that the murderer is here in this house. What if he decides to kill somebody else?"

I shivered and moved closer to Lucy. "Don't let yourself

think like that," I said. "You're perfectly safe. You're not playing the game Mr. Trevor set up. If anyone is in danger, it's bound to be one of the game-players."

"That's not what Walter said," Lucy told me, and her eyes were as round as the curve of her cheeks and face. "We all know that you're the one who's got that special clue that gives you more information than the rest of them put together. If somebody else is going to be killed, it's very likely to be *you*!"

NINE

I had to get out of that dark hallway and away from Lucy, so I ran all the way down the stairs and into the sun-room.

I took the only empty chair. It was one of the hard, straight-backed chairs, but I didn't mind. I tried not to stare as I examined each face. Alex's expression was blank, Julia's was puzzled, and Thea's was concerned; but the other three were steaming. Something had really made them angry. I kept in mind that one of these people was a murderer. One of them had searched my room. And, according to Walter's way of thinking, one of them might be after me!

"Are you feeling well, Samantha?" Aunt Thea asked. "You look a little flushed."

"I'm okay," I told her, and—even though my fingers trembled—I managed to flip some pages over the top of my writing pad until I reached a clean sheet of paper. "What kind of clues have we got this time?"

"Clues?" Laura threw her sheet of paper at me. It

landed at my feet, and I bent to pick it up. "These aren't clues! They're just more of Augustus's nasty comments!"

On her sheet of paper was typed SHE LAID AN EGG, AND IT WAS A DOOZY.

I had to agree with Laura that the statement wasn't very nice. She must have been unhappy enough about the bad reviews of her past two movies. She didn't need an amateur critic's report.

"What Augustus wrote to me isn't flattering either," Senator Maggio said, "and I have no idea why he had to drag my family into this."

"What does your clue say?" I asked.

As a pulse pounded in his neck and his face darkened, the senator read, " 'THE BALD EAGLE HAS MANY KIN.' " He gave me the paper, leaned back, and self-consciously ran the palm of one hand over the top of his smooth, shining head.

"At least he didn't take potshots at your love life," Buck muttered. "It isn't Augustus's business or anyone else's that Eloise and I are . . . well, having a trial separation."

"Is that what your clue says?" I asked. This wasn't making sense.

"Here," Buck said, "read it yourself," and he handed it to me.

In the middle of the paper was typed SHE IS LOST AND GONE FOREVER. DREADFUL SORRY, PAPPY.

"Did your wife call you 'pappy'?" I asked Buck after I'd read his clue aloud.

"No," he said. "No one ever has. We don't have children."

"Maybe this isn't about your wife. Maybe it means something else."

"Oh, sure. What else *could* it mean?"

I shifted in my chair, which wasn't terribly comfortable, and answered, "I know this sounds crazy, but while I was reading the first part of your clue a tune came into my head. Don't you remember that old song? I think I learned it at Girl Scout summer camp, or maybe it was in kindergarten." I sang, " 'Oh my darling, oh my darling, oh my darling Clementine. She is lost and gone forever, dreadful sorry, Clementine.' "

"Is your wife's name Clementine?" Laura asked Buck.

"No, it isn't," Buck snapped, and his forehead crinkled into a couple of deep creases as he tried to think things out.

Thea suddenly broke in. "If Buck's clue came from a song, then I'm wondering if mine did, as well." She read, " 'DARLING, I AM GROWING OLD,' " then dropped her paper into her lap.

"That's a song, Aunt Thea?"

"Long ago it was a very popular song," she said. "It begins like this: 'Darling, I am growing old. Silver threads among the gold shine upon my brow today; life is fading fast away.' "

Totally depressing, I thought, *and people complain about* our *music!*

"Oooh, what about this?" Laura asked. "What if it's a prophecy of his own death."

"Nonsense," Senator Maggio complained. "It's just more of this stupid foolishness we've been forced into."

Alex gave his paper to me. "Two of the clues may be tied in to songs, but I doubt if mine is. It makes no sense whatsoever."

I read aloud what was typed on Alex's paper: " 'IT WASN'T ENTIRELY JASON'S FAULT.' "

I asked Alex, "Who's Jason?"

Alex shrugged. "I have no idea. I don't know a Jason."

"Jason's a common enough name," Julia told him. "Think about it. The *Jason* Augustus referred to wouldn't have to be a friend. Maybe he's a neighbor or a business associate."

Alex looked at her sharply. "What do you mean by that?"

Julia's eyes widened. "I don't mean anything. I thought we were supposed to try to work out these clues."

"We haven't heard yours," I told her.

"Right," Julia said, and sighed. "Perhaps I'm being oversensitive, but I think my clue also comes under the insult category." She read, " 'TAKE A LITTLE SOMETHING FROM OLIVER, THE POET.' "

"Take what?" Buck asked. "What could you take from a poet?"

"His words," I said.

"I don't get it."

"She means plagiarize," the senator grumbled.

"That's silly," Laura said as Julia's face became blotched with pink. "Julia doesn't write poetry." Laura tilted her head to one side and asked, "Who is this Oliver, anyway?"

"I don't know," Julia said, still embarrassed. "I don't *read* poetry, either."

Buck suddenly got to his feet. "None of this stuff makes sense to me. There's only one thing left to do and that's search this house from top to bottom, and I say we start with Trevor's room."

"Wait a minute," I complained. "This isn't your house!"

"It's all right, Samantha," Thea said. "We must do everything we can in order to try to find the manuscript before . . ."

She didn't finish the sentence, but she didn't have to. The rest of it would have been "before the police arrive."

"I'll go with you," Senator Maggio said, and he tried to match Buck's long strides in an attempt to catch up.

Alex slowly unfolded himself and got to his feet. "I'm going to do a little searching myself," he admitted, and chuckled. "Maybe the butler's pantry. Remember the old saying 'The butler did it'? And a thorough search of the wine cellar might be a good idea."

"What about going through Augustus's desk?" Julia asked him. "Because . . . well, because the body was there, we didn't look very carefully the first time. I'll go with you."

"You don't have to," Alex said. "I prefer to work alone."

"You made that pretty obvious when you kept those clues for yourself, and because of that I don't trust you for a minute!" Julia shouted.

Alex just shrugged. "That makes it mutual," he said, "especially after the sneaky insinuation you made about my business associates."

"What insinuation?" Julia's anger turned to surprise.

Alex didn't answer, so before Julia could continue the argument, I broke in. "You asked me to try to solve these clues, but you're all leaving. I'm going to need help."

Even though all of Augustus's guests—even Aunt Thea —wanted to find the manuscript to destroy it, and I wanted to find it to see if it would give away the identity of the murderer, I needed other thoughts and viewpoints. I wished Darlene were on hand.

Laura shook her head and walked to the doorway. "I wouldn't be any help at all," she said. "The clues are much too confusing. I've got a terrible headache anyway, so I'm going to my room and take a nap."

Julia and Alex, in spite of their differences, left the sunroom together, Laura trailing behind.

Thea motioned me to join her on one of the wicker couches. "I'll do what I can to help you," she said, "but I must be honest with you, Samantha. I believe that the clues may be unsolvable. It would be typical of Augustus to offer false promises just to enjoy watching the discomfort of his guests. I'm afraid that whatever he wrote about us in his manuscript is there to stay."

"Aunt Thea," I asked, "was he always that mean?"

She shook her head. "We had many happy days together when we were young. I made sure his working days were quiet and comfortable, and when we traveled and partied there were always exciting people to meet and interesting things to do."

"I saw the pictures in the Kings' Corner," I told her. "But you weren't in them. Only Augustus."

"Being photographed with royalty was important to Augustus. My presence in the photographs wasn't necessary." For a moment she was silent, then said, "Augustus could be tender and affectionate when he wanted to be, and when he wasn't . . . I accepted it as part of his genius."

"But you fell out of love with him, didn't you?" I asked.

"I suppose so."

"Was he ill? Is that why he became mean?"

"He had bouts of pain, but that was no excuse. There are many people who become gentler through suffering."

"Then why didn't you leave him, Aunt Thea? Why did you stay holed up in this house, away from everything?"

"Marriage is a contract," Thea said, but she looked away from me, and I knew she hadn't given me the right answer. Augustus had been holding something over her head, and it had to be whatever he'd written about in his latest manuscript.

In the silence that followed I listened to the steady drumming of the rain and its gulping gurgles as it rushed through the drain spouts, splashing on the concrete walk-ways and patios. The storm was no longer violent, but the rain continued to come down as if it would never end.

I stared down at my note pad where I'd copied down *Game Clues* #3:

SHE LAID AN EGG, AND IT WAS A DOOZY	L.
THE BALD EAGLE HAS MANY KIN	M.
SHE IS LOST AND GONE FOREVER. DREADFUL SORRY, PAPPY	B.
DARLING, I AM GROWING OLD	T.
IT WASN'T ENTIRELY JASON'S FAULT	A.
TAKE A LITTLE SOMETHING FROM OLIVER, THE POET	J.

When I was younger, I had thought I was pretty good at making up clues with Darlene and solving them, and I wanted to prove I could still do it, so I refused to give up as easily as the others had. "I'd really like to work on these awhile, Aunt Thea," I said.

"Of course," she answered. "As I told you earlier, I'll help you, but I have no idea how to start."

Could I trust her? I had to. Besides, she was my mother's aunt. "If these are legitimate clues, then each set has to have something in common," I explained. "Nobody wanted to tell me what was in the first set, so I don't know what they were all about. But in the second set we were told that 'one will be above all.' I can only guess that it means the king."

"Arthur insisted it was the ace."

"But you and Augustus played cribbage. There was even a cribbage board in his office. I think he would have thought of the king as top card, and put in the ace just to lead astray all the bridge players."

She smiled. "I'm inclined to agree with you. What else do you get from that set of clues?"

"Nothing," I said. "Just *kings*. Although *king* could mean *ruler* or *general* or *official* or *emperor* or whatever might be in that line."

Wait a minute! I thought. *Kings' Corner*. But there was no place among those photographs to hide a manuscript, and I didn't see how the pictures could give me any kind of help in solving the clue.

Thea said, "Samantha, you saw the first clue that Augustus gave me. It was a travel brochure to Acapulco."

"That's all?"

"That's all."

"But what does it mean? You told me you'd figured it out."

"Wasn't it Julia who told you that these were more messages than clues? That they were Augustus's way of informing us that he had uncovered our secrets. You don't need them to solve the puzzle, Samantha. Please believe me."

While I was thinking about it and deciding that I had to believe Aunt Thea, Mrs. Engstrom came into the room with a teapot and two cups and saucers. "Hot tea tastes good on a rainy day," she said, and gave careful scrutiny to Thea. "Are you feeling well, Mrs. Trevor? I'm sure that this stress is tiring you."

"I'm fine, thank you," Thea said. "There's no need to worry about me."

"I'll be glad when this storm is over," Mrs. Engstrom said as she poured two cups of tea. "Tomás is upset because he's running low on sugar and salad greens and I can't send in my computer order. I wouldn't dare turn on my computer with only the generator to power it."

"How do you shop by computer?" I asked.

"A number of people on the island have a software program with a grocer in Avalon," Thea answered. "We send an order on our household computer, he receives it, and either delivers it or it's ready when we pick it up."

"Well, latest reports on the radio are that the storm should be over by Monday," Mrs. Engstrom said.

I could hear the relief in her voice, but Thea and I glanced at each other with concern. Even though we had different reasons for wanting to find that manuscript, we both realized that we hadn't much time.

Mrs. Engstrom caught the look and asked, "How far have you come on working out the clues, Miss Burns?"

"Not very," I answered.

"Does 'not very' instead of 'no' mean that you've begun to solve it?"

I opened my mouth to say "yes," but thought how weak my guess was on the second set of clues and how I hadn't even begun on the third, so after hesitating just a fraction too long I answered, "No, I haven't."

She stared at me as though she suspected I'd just lied to her, and walked to the other side of the room, where she busied herself straightening magazines and picking up a couple of empty cups that had been left on a side table.

Thea sipped at her tea and said, "Look over your list, Samantha. If you have any questions, just ask, and maybe between us we can come up with the answers."

"Thanks," I said, so grateful for her moral support and so sure she couldn't possibly be the murderer that I confided, "Aunt Thea, I have to find this manuscript before the others do."

"No, Samantha," she said quietly.

"Don't you see, Aunt Thea? If we read the manuscript, we might find out who the murderer is."

"If we read the manuscript, six lives might be ruined."

I squirmed uncomfortably. "But not yours, Aunt Thea."

"Yes, mine too," she answered.

I shouldn't have spilled everything out. I looked around to see if we might have been overheard, but Thea and I were alone. Not knowing what to say next, I got up and went to the desk, opening the lined pad to the page with the number-three clues and spread my notes next to it. I couldn't look at Thea. I didn't want to do anything that might hurt her, but surely she had to understand that someone in this house was a killer and might kill again!

From the corner of my eye I saw her refill her teacup. "I'll wait right here with you, dear," she said, as though our conversation about the manuscript hadn't happened. "If you want my help for anything, just ask."

"Thank you, Aunt Thea," I murmured, and set to work.

I read the clues over twice, and each time I came to a dead stop on Julia's clue. Finally, I looked up at Thea and said, "Do you know any poets named Oliver? The only Oliver I can think of was in that novel *Oliver Twist* by Charles Dickens, and that Oliver was a kid, not a poet."

"We can use the encyclopedia in Augustus's office," she suggested.

"I thought of that," I said, shuddering at the idea of going back into that room, "but it's going to be almost impossible to check out poets by first names."

Thea smiled. "I can give you a start," she said. "What about Oliver Goldsmith, the British poet who lived in the seventeen hundreds? You've studied *The Deserted Village* in school, haven't you?"

"No," I said, "but I like the title. Is it a mystery novel?"

"It's a poem, and I do believe I still remember a few lines from those I once had to memorize about the village schoolmaster." She got a faraway look in her eyes and recited, " 'But past is all his fame. The very spot where many a time he triumphed is forgot.' "

She could have been talking about Augustus. We both felt the impact of the words at the same time and looked away from each other, embarrassed.

I wrote down *Goldsmith* and went on to Buck's clue, writing down the chorus of "My Darling Clementine" and snatches of words from the verses. I could only remember part of them, and I couldn't remember any that had the word *pappy* in them. Aunt Thea had remembered that awful old song about growing old, so I asked, "Do you remember any of the words of 'My Darling Clementine'?"

She put down her teacup and hummed quietly to herself before she answered, "Just snatches."

"Do you remember anything about Clementine's pappy?"

Between her eyebrows a little crease flickered as she thought. "I can't remember him being called *pappy*. Wasn't he a miner?"

"Right," I said. " 'Came a miner, a forty-niner, and his daughter Clementine.' " As I wrote it down I wondered aloud, "So far, this stuff is pretty gloomy. We've got somebody growing old." I checked my notes. "With 'life fading fast away.' Then we've got somebody being forgotten after he dies, and now old Clementine being lost and gone forever. Augustus didn't look on the bright side, did he?"

I got another thought, and this one was too scary to share with Aunt Thea. Was Augustus warning each of his guests that something bad was going to happen to them? And if he was, when was it going to happen? With the weekend half over, we wouldn't have to wait long to find out!

TEN

*D*on't think like that!* I cautioned myself. *He's not here to do anything to us, even if he wanted to.* But the memory of his body upstairs in the bathtub was so unnerving that I pushed back my chair and stood up.

"Are you through working on clues already?" Aunt Thea asked.

"Oh, no," I said. "I've made a good start, with your help, Aunt Thea, but I've got some questions to ask two of the others."

"What kind of questions?"

I knew Aunt Thea wasn't prying. She was just being interested. "Well," I said, "I've been thinking that the solution to Laura's clue might be in the name of one of the movies that flopped so badly. I don't remember either of them. Do you?"

"No," she said. "Better ask Laura."

"I have something to ask Senator Maggio, too—the

names of all his relatives. Maybe their initials spell something. I won't know unless I try."

" 'The bald eagle has many kin,' " Thea said.

"You've got a good memory," I told her.

Her smile was sorrowful. "Under the circumstances, the clues would be hard to forget."

I took my pen and pad, with my notes stuffed inside, and headed for the stairway. But I glanced into the parlor and saw Senator Maggio standing alone at the window, staring out at the rain.

As I passed the Kings' Corner I paused to study the framed photographs, but pairs of eyes stared blankly out at me, offering nothing.

The senator didn't acknowledge me as I joined him, and I supposed he was drawn into that swirl of gray sky and grayer sea, its choppy surface shredded by rain and wind.

I waited patiently, then said, "Could I ask you a question, Senator Maggio?"

"If you wish." His voice was as depressed as the view outside the window.

"Okay," I said. "It's about your relatives." But I was sidetracked by my next thought. "Weren't you searching the house for the manuscript?"

"I don't see any hope of finding it before the storm lets up," he answered.

"Then help me solve the clues."

He shook his head. "I don't see how that can be accomplished either."

"Let's try. Why don't you tell me the names of your relatives?"

He turned toward me, startled, but then relaxed. "Oh.

You're referring to the bald eagle's many kin. Frankly, there aren't that many, but I'll go through the list."

He told me the names of his wife, his two brothers, his son and daughter and their spouses, and his two little granddaughters. He reached for his wallet, and I thought for a moment he was going to show me their pictures again, but apparently he decided not to and let his hands drop to his sides, once again staring out the window.

"Everyone makes mistakes," the senator said, so softly that at first I wasn't sure he was talking to me. "Why can't they be forgotten? Why should such a terrible price have to be paid?"

"He didn't know he'd have to pay it."

Again he turned to me, an expression of surprise on his face. "I was talking about past mistakes made by the guests who've been invited here."

"I thought you were talking about Augustus Trevor."

Senator Maggio shook his head. "He's the one responsible for all this trouble."

I nodded. "And he's the one who made the biggest mistake. He invited a murderer to his house."

"You'd better keep in mind," he said quietly, "that the murderer is still present."

I wasn't comfortable about the forbidding look on his face, so I left him in a hurry and trotted upstairs to see if Laura would answer my questions.

On the landing I took time to glance at the names of Senator Maggio's relatives, but they added up to zilch. Except for the first letter of his son's first name (Arthur Maggio, Jr.), the others were just a jumble of consonants: two *J*'s, two *K*'s, two *M*'s, one *P*, and one *H*. I not only couldn't make anything out of it, it occurred to me that I'd hardly call this "many kin." I probably expected something like one of those family reunion photos in which relatives are fanned out all over the porch and lawn. Senator Maggio's clue had to mean something else. But what?

The back of my neck prickled, as though someone were watching me, but I looked all around and couldn't see anyone. The burial urn on the stand caught my eye, and I whispered to whatever invisible something that might happen to be hanging around it, "I'm working as hard as I can to get us all out of here in one piece. Be patient, will you? And stop staring!"

I found Laura Reed just where she said she'd be—in her bedroom, but she hadn't been napping. When she opened the door to my knock, her eyes were red, and there were drippy mascara smudges on her cheeks.

"Help me solve the clues," I said.

She shrugged as she stood aside to let me in. "I haven't the foggiest notion how to go about it."

"Well, I do. I mean, it isn't foggy. I want to ask you about your last two films."

Laura perched on the edge of the bed—a high four-poster covered with a dark blue-green quilted spread. There was a heavy swag of the same material over the head of the bed, caught into a kind of gold-colored crown, and at the windows there were draperies to match. Maybe when the sun was out the room didn't look so gloomy. I was beginning to wonder if the person who decorated this house had learned his profession in Dracula's castle.

"I should remember, but I don't," I said as I sat in a narrow gilt chair that stood in front of a dressing table. "What were the names of your last two films?"

"Nobody remembers," Laura said, and she slumped,

hugging her elbows. "Last year was *Daughter of Vengeance*. The year before that was *Lady in Trouble*." She sighed. "Prophetic, wasn't it? This lady's really in trouble."

I wrote down the titles and looked up. "Maybe not."

She sighed again, a long, dramatic sigh that seemed to come all the way from her toes. "It wasn't murder," she said. "It was a moment of anger, of acting without thinking. It was an accident."

I gulped. "Are you telling me you killed Augustus Trevor?"

Her green-gold eyes glowed like spotlights as she turned them on me. "Of course not, because I didn't. I wasn't even talking about Augustus."

"Then who . . . ?"

"What difference does it make? This is all such a hodgepodge, and my head hurts so much, I don't even remember what we were talking about."

I felt cold all the way to my toes. "You'd said you were in trouble, and then you talked about the murder . . . I mean the way it took place, as though you'd been there . . . and . . . well, it just seemed to fit."

No matter what Laura said or denied saying, she certainly had had the opportunity to kill him.

"Never mind. Forget what I said. I was just thinking out loud." She sat up straighter. "We'll talk about your clues. How do the names of my films fit into them?"

"I don't know yet," I said.

"Augustus makes me absolutely furious," she snapped. "Telling me I laid an egg and it was a doozy! How rude can you get?"

"Maybe he didn't mean you," I told her.

The corners of her mouth turned down, and her voice

was sarcastic. "Oh? Who else but an actor lays an egg? Are you talking about a chicken? A goose? Maybe the goose that laid the golden egg. Wouldn't Augustus think that was a great joke."

A knock at the door made us jump.

Laura opened it to Lucy, who had brought two extra pillows. Laura thanked her, shut the door again, and tossed the pillows onto the bed. "I sleep better with lots and lots of pillows," she told me, but as she sank back onto the bed she became plaintive. "I really don't expect to sleep at all—not until that manuscript is found and destroyed."

Tears glistened again in her eyes as she told me, "I hunted over every inch of this room, even between the mattress and springs. There's a vent into the attic from the closet in my room. I even checked that."

"Maybe we'll solve this puzzle and find the manuscript," I told her.

"How far have you come in solving the clues?"

"Not very."

She drooped again, reminding me of a fading petunia on a wobbly stem. "Wouldn't it be nice," she asked, "if we could live our lives over again and take out all the bad parts?"

"I guess so," I answered, although I'd been lucky enough not to have many bad parts and nothing so terrible that I'd want to live my life over again to miss it.

"If I weren't so miserable, I'd be bored to death here," Laura said, and looked at her watch. "Do you realize it's more than an hour until dinnertime?"

"I've been thinking about it in the opposite way," I answered. "The weekend and the storm will be over soon.

The time we have left to find the manuscript is running out."

Laura groaned. "You came here to cheer me up. Right?"

A loud knock on the door startled us, but we heard Buck call, "It's me, Buck. Wake up, Laura. Open the door."

Laura opened it graciously, holding her head high, as though she were a queen. "I wasn't sleeping," she said. "And you don't need to shout."

"Sorry," he said, and his feet did a kind of fumbling shuffle as he stepped into the room. "This whole thing has got me so riled, it's made me do things I never thought I'd ever do."

"Like what?" I asked, and held my breath, waiting for his answer.

He looked at me with surprise, and I realized he hadn't known I was with Laura. "Like pawing through people's things, searching for that manuscript."

I relaxed. What had I expected? That he'd confess to committing murder?

He nodded toward the legal pad on my lap. "Are you getting anywhere with those clues?"

"Not yet," I admitted, "but I'm trying. That's why I'm here. I was asking Laura some questions about her clue, and I'd like to talk to you about yours, too, if you've got a few minutes."

Buck made a scrunched-up face that answered my question. "I've been going room to room," he said. "I want to search Laura's room too."

"Forget it," she said. "I already searched it."

His eyes narrowed as he studied her. "Did you find anything?"

"Of course not. Don't you think I'd have told everybody if I did?"

Buck didn't answer right away, and Laura's neck and face flushed an angry red. "You don't trust me? You think I'd hold out?"

"I don't know who to trust," he mumbled. "All I know is that somebody here killed Augustus."

Her voice rose to a screech. "You think it was me? How about you? Maybe *you* murdered him!"

"Okay, maybe I did!" he yelled back.

"You did?" I whispered, and clutched the arm of the little dressing table chair.

"No, I didn't. I was just making a point. Any one of us could be the murderer, so who are we going to trust?"

"Please sit down, just for a minute," I begged. "I've got only a couple of questions for you. I need to know how the song 'My Darling Clementine' fits into your life."

"Fits into my life? That's a stupid question. The answer is that it doesn't."

"Maybe I didn't ask my question the right way," I said, and felt myself blush. "I meant, was it a special song for you? Did you hear it at some time under special circumstances?"

"No," he said. I wished he'd sit down. He was awfully big to glower down on an innocent bystander—me.

"You know the words to the song, don't you?"

He shrugged. "A few words, here and there, that's all."

"Okay, what does 'pappy' mean to you?"

"Beats me. I didn't call my dad 'pappy.' I don't even know anyone called 'pappy.' "

"You're with kids a lot. As you said, you're a role model. Maybe sometime in your past—"

Buck interrupted. "What are you getting at?"

Like a ferocious pit bull, he leaned toward me, eyes glinting in narrow slits, his lower lip curled outward. He scared me so much I jumped out of my chair.

"N-nothing!" I stuttered. "I—I'm just trying to figure out these clues!"

He didn't believe me. Not for a minute. He took a step toward me, and I shrank back against the dressing table, terrified of what he'd say next. But just then we heard muffled footsteps running toward us, and the door was jerked open.

Julia poked her head inside, stared from Laura to Buck to me, and said, "Come on downstairs. Make it quick! I've found the fourth set of clues!"

ELEVEN

"**W**here did you find them?" everyone asked Julia, and as soon as we were all seated in the sun-room, she told us.

"The envelopes were fastened with a rubber band and tucked at the very back in the middle drawer of Augustus's desk under some papers." When no one said anything for a few moments, Julia's voice rose. "Don't look at me as though you think I'm lying. We didn't search that part of the desk this morning. Remember? And we weren't looking for clues. We were looking for the manuscript."

"Julia's right," Buck said. "I went through the drawers on each side, but I couldn't . . . that is, Augustus was . . ."

"Wait a minute," I said. "The first clues he handed out. The second were under his arm, ready to be given out the next morning. But why would Alex have found the third set in Augustus's bedroom, and then this set—"

Alex interrupted. "I didn't find them in his bedroom. I

found them just inside the middle desk drawer in his office." He shrugged. "I suppose if I'd been able to check the back of the drawer I would have found the fourth set of clues."

I felt cold and creepy as the thought hit me. "Were you looking in the desk while Augustus was still . . . ?"

"It's none of your business," Alex said.

"He was *dead*," Laura whispered.

"There's no point wasting time with this discussion," Senator Maggio argued. "Will you please give us our envelopes?"

Julia proceeded to do so, and I saw that on the top of each envelope, next to the players' names, had been printed in that same bright blue ink, *Game Clue* #4.

It was hard to be patient while the suspects—as I thought of them—read their clues to themselves. I wished I had elbowed in on the couch next to Laura, but I was sitting cross-legged on the floor, which was more comfortable than the hard straight-backed chair which had been the only seat left.

Alex was the first to speak. "This clue makes no more sense than the others," he said, and read, " 'MORE SILENT THAN THE TOMBS ARE.' "

I began to write it down but looked up, startled, as Laura burst into tears. "That dreadful, horrible man," she sobbed.

Her clue fluttered from her fingers as she covered her eyes, and I picked it up. On the paper was typed LIKE DAVY JONES'S LOCKER—MINUS THE SEA.

As soon as Aunt Thea calmed Laura down, I asked her if I could read her clue to the others.

Laura lay back against the cushions, one hand pressed

against her forehead, and said, "Oh, go ahead. What difference does it make now?"

I read Laura's clue, then asked Senator Maggio, "What does yours say?"

He shrugged. "I suppose it's a threat: 'DEADER THAN A DOORNAIL, GREEN AS A PEA.'"

Julia's eyes widened. "These are all about death. Listen to mine: 'TEA AND SYMPATHY—DONE TO DEATH.'"

"So that's what this means. I thought—" Buck interrupted himself and read: "'WHY A SUDDEN DEATH PLAY?'"

"My clue is in line with the others," Thea told us. She handed me her paper, and I read aloud, "'GIVE UP THE GHOST.'"

With tears in her eyes she said, "Please believe me when I tell you that I have no idea what Augustus had in mind. To bring you here, to force you into playing this horrible game, and then to threaten all of you—all of *us*—with death, is unbelievable to me. I'm sorry. I'm so terribly sorry."

"No one blames you, Thea," Julia told her, and the others murmured in agreement.

Thea was sitting close enough to me so that I could reach out and take her hand. "Aunt Thea," I said, "you're forgetting that these aren't messages Augustus was giving you. They're clues, which means they're supposed to add up to something else."

Everyone stared at me. Since they were all seated on chairs, and I was cross-legged on the floor, I felt like the frog in biology class just before the teacher gets ready to dissect him. I quickly stood up and read aloud the clues I'd written down:

MORE SILENT THAN THE TOMBS ARE	A.
LIKE DAVY JONES'S LOCKER—MINUS THE SEA	L.
DEADER THAN A DOORNAIL, GREEN AS A PEA	M.
TEA AND SYMPATHY—DONE TO DEATH	J.
WHY A SUDDEN DEATH PLAY?	B.
GIVE UP THE GHOST	T.

As I heard them I got a strange feeling. Something about these clues was odd. For an instant I was almost able to grasp the reason, but I looked the list over again and the feeling had gone. I said to the others, "As I already told you, there has to be a common theme in these clues. That's the way it works. Why don't we get busy and try to find it?"

Laura moaned and staggered to her feet. "It's not true it's not true it's not true!" she gurgled as a fresh burst of tears poured down her cheeks. She pushed her way out of the circle of chairs and ran out of the room.

"There's no use in any of this." Buck's voice was deep with despair. He slowly hoisted himself out of his chair and walked away.

Alex stood and stretched before he said to me, "If you can make anything out of 'more silent than the tombs are,' I'll believe it when I see it."

"If *I* can? How about you? You're the ones who were supposed to figure out the clues and solve them," I told him. "Don't leave it all up to me. I need help."

"Don't we all," Alex said, and left the group.

"Come on," I told the others. "Help me figure out what all this stuff means."

"You said there was a common theme, didn't you?" Senator Maggio asked.

"Yes."

"Well, it's clear. The theme is death."

"No," I insisted. "That's too obvious. There has to be another meaning."

The senator didn't like to be contradicted. The expression on his face was unmistakable.

As he stalked out of the room Julia said, "I'll help you, Sam."

"So will I," Thea added. "What do you want us to do?"

"Help me look for hidden meanings in these clues."

"Let's start with mine," Julia said. *Tea and Sympathy* is the title of a novel, and it was made into a movie."

"Anything else here that ties in with a book or a movie?" I asked.

We studied the list but came up with zilch.

"There's a clue about football and a clue about sailors," I said. "At least I think Davy Jones was a sailor, wasn't he?"

Julia half rose out of her chair. "Wait a minute! Locker! Davy Jones's locker!"

"Aunt Thea!" I cried out. "Could the manuscript be hidden in a locker?"

Thea looked bewildered and spread out her hands helplessly. "We don't have anything resembling a locker here," she said.

"What about down at the dock? Are there lockers there for gear or equipment?"

"No. There's a large metal chest in the boat shed where equipment for the boats is kept, but the crew members live in the house for employees and keep their gear there."

"Where is this house?" Julia asked.

"Just the other side of the cove."

"All your employees live there?"

"Yes." Thea nodded, then suddenly said, "Except for Mrs. Engstrom, of course. I guess I think of her as more of a friend than an employee. She has a small suite of first-floor rooms here in our home."

Julia thought a moment, then asked, "Is it possible that Augustus hid the other copy of his manuscript in the employees' house?"

"I know he didn't," Thea told her. "During the last few years Augustus became sedentary and rarely went outdoors. I'm positive that Augustus didn't leave the house at any time after he completed his manuscript."

"What if he gave the manuscript to one of the employees to hide? Maybe Walter?" I asked.

Thea shook her head. "Mrs. Engstrom informed me that she immediately questioned Tomás, Lucy, and Walter. They knew nothing about a copy of the manuscript. In fact, they're all frightened about everything that has happened."

"I'd still feel better if we searched the other house," Julia said.

Thea stood, her spine as straight and stiff as the back of the chair she'd been sitting in. "I can't allow anyone to invade my employees' privacy," she said. "However, if you wish, I will ask Walter and one of the others—Buck, perhaps—if they would like to put on raincoats and boots and climb down to the boat shed in order to search the chest." She paused and glanced at the windows, which were blurred with a steady shimmer of rain. As she turned back to Julia, Thea said, "Maybe *you'd* like to visit the boat shed, Julia."

"Well . . ." Julia drew out the word. Her gaze was on the windows. "If no one else volunteers, I'll go."

"I'll ask them," Thea said, and left the room.

Julia slumped against the arm of the couch and pressed her fingertips over her eyes. "It's never worth it," she mumbled. "Nothing is."

"Worth what?" I asked.

She slid her hands down her face and let them fall into her lap as she looked at me. "Peace of mind," she said. "I gave it up too easily."

I didn't want to intrude on her thoughts, but I didn't understand what she was talking about, so I asked, "How did you give it up?"

"With one stroke I traded it for a handful of beans—magic beans." Her laugh was scary because there was no humor in it.

One stroke? Only too clearly I could visualize Augustus Trevor's bloody head. Even though Julia and I were alone in the sun-room, which was growing darker and gloomier by the minute, I blurted out, "Are you talking about Augustus Trevor's murder?"

For a moment Julia looked confused, but as she understood my question she leaned forward, her gaze as penetrating as a laser beam. "Are you asking if I killed Augustus?" she whispered.

"Uh—not exactly. I—I don't know what to think."

"Then I'll tell you what to think." She moved even closer, and her eyes glittered. "Don't try getting inside other people's minds. Don't begin suspecting them, and above all, don't tell other people your suspicions or you might very well find yourself in real trouble."

* * *

Buck and Walter did go down to the boat shed, and they came back to report that, just as Thea had told us, there was nothing but equipment in the metal chest. Buck hadn't been able to fit his overly long feet into any of the work boots on the back porch, and the slicker they crammed him into couldn't fasten across his chest, so he was as grumbly cross as a cold, wet bulldog.

"We haven't much time left in which to find the manuscript," Alex said. "As long as Buck has survived the elements on this first trip, it might be a good idea if he made his way over to the employees' house and took a look around."

"Yeah? What about *you* going out in that mess, instead of me?" Growling as drops trickled from his scalp down his face and neck, Buck grabbed a fistful of Alex's shirt, and for a moment I held my breath, sure that Buck was going to hit Alex.

But Buck suddenly flung Alex backward. Alex sprawled on the sofa, then slid to the floor, while Buck stomped toward the stairs. Alex didn't say a word. He climbed to his feet, methodically rearranged his open collar, tucked his shirt back into his slacks, and walked toward the dining room.

Buck was a very strong man, and he had a temper. Could he have gone to Augustus's office and argued with him? Could he have lost his temper and hit Augustus?

Maybe.

I gathered up my writing pad, the loose papers, and the pen and walked to the parlor. I had a new idea about the photographs in the Kings' Corner. What if a message was tucked inside one of the frames behind the backing? I could hardly wait to find out.

Someone else had been even more impatient. The photos, cardboard, glass, and frames had been separated and were strewn all over the table. What a mess! I was furious at this crude violation of someone else's property, and more than a little angry that whoever had done this had got the idea of searching the photos before I had.

I didn't try to repair the damage. Only Aunt Thea would know which photo went with which frame. I found a seat at a small antique desk in the parlor. I turned on the small green-globed desk lamp and moved a lot of little china and crystal birds, which were arranged in groups on top of the desk, so I'd have room to work. I spread out my sheets of paper and went back to the third set of clues, writing down everything that came to mind. I checked to see if the first letter of each sentence added up to anything, but it didn't, which didn't surprise me. Augustus had planned some tough clues, and he wouldn't waste his time with an easy kid trick. The clues had to have a common theme, and I was determined to find it.

"Samantha."

I hadn't heard anyone come into the room, and I wasn't expecting Alex to speak my name just behind my left ear, so I let out a yelp and jumped up, my papers scattered around me.

"How long have you been looking over my shoulder?" I demanded.

"Not long. I came to see how you were doing."

"You didn't have to sneak up on me!"

"I wasn't sneaking. The carpets are soft. It wasn't my fault that you didn't hear me come in."

I picked up my papers, and tried to look dignified. "Sorry," I muttered. No matter what excuse Alex gave, I still believed he'd been sneaking, but I had to answer his question. "I haven't got any answers yet, if that's what you want to know."

"You've made a lot of notes. May I see them?"

He reached for the papers, and I instinctively drew back.

"What's the matter?" Alex asked. "I thought you said you wanted help. Don't you trust me?"

"No, I don't," I answered. "You opened the third set of clues and tried to solve them yourself." I glanced across the room at the Kings' Corner. "And you're probably the one who took apart all the framed photographs of Augustus with the kings."

Alex shrugged. "So what if I did? There weren't any rules to the game, or instructions to share information. We were simply told to find the treasure and win."

Curiosity took over. "Did you find anything in the photos?"

"No." Alex took the papers out of my hand and I let him. He walked to one of the sofas, sat down, and laid the sheets of paper on the coffee table. I sat next to him and waited while he read every one of my notes.

When he'd finished, he turned and looked right into my eyes. "You made these notes earlier. I watched you. What else have you come up with?"

"Nothing," I said. I wished he wouldn't stare at me like that. I felt as though he were poking around in my brain looking for answers.

"You still don't trust me," Alex murmured.

I inched a little farther away on the sofa as I said, "One person in this house is a murderer, so why should I trust any of you?"

"I didn't kill Augustus," he said, "so it's perfectly safe for you to trust me." His lips stretched into a broad smile, but his eyes were cold.

Alex waited for my answer, but I didn't say a word. I couldn't.

His smile snapped off like a door being slammed, and he got to his feet. "Very well then," he said. "I'll work alone."

As he walked toward the door I jumped up and called, "Wait a minute. Give back my notes."

"No," he said, and that awful smile crept back to his face again. "I figured out what you're doing, Samantha. You want to find the manuscript before the rest of us do because you probably have some odd idea that by reading it you might discover the identity of the murderer, but I'm not going to let you. No matter what I have to do to stop you, I'm going to find that manuscript first!"

TWELVE

I was afraid of Alex, much too afraid to make a scene about my notes being stolen, and I convinced myself that losing the clues didn't make that much difference. I had worked so long on the clues, I had memorized them, so I took three clean sheets of paper and jotted the clues down again under *Game Clues* #2, *Game Clues* #3, and *Game Clues* #4.

The notes, however, didn't come back to mind as easily. I remembered the words of that yucky song Aunt Thea sang about growing old with silver threads among the gold, and I wrote down Oliver's last name, Goldsmith. What else had I jotted down?

Thea called to me from the doorway, and as she briskly came toward me she said, "Samantha, I thought of something that might help with Alex's clue about Jason. Wasn't it something like not blaming Jason because it wasn't his fault?"

I read from the clues: " 'It wasn't entirely Jason's fault.' "

"I have an idea," Thea said, and beamed. "Jason and Medea. Remember the tale? Medea urged Jason to steal her father's golden fleece. What was her father's name . . . ? King . . . oh, dear. Do you remember?"

"Not at the moment," I said, but as I wrote down the sentence I began to get an excited bubbling in my stomach. It was the way I used to feel when I was coming close to working out the answer to some really hard puzzle Darlene had dreamed up for me.

"Do Jason and Medea fit in?" Thea asked.

Did they fit! The pieces of this puzzle began to come together, and in my excitement I gripped the edge of the table. "I don't know yet," I mumbled, and couldn't meet Thea's eyes. "They might. Thanks."

Thea was Mom's aunt, so why couldn't I trust her enough to tell her that she may have given me the answer to solving the third set of clues? What was the matter with me?

I had just opened my mouth to spill the whole thing when Laura appeared in the doorway, looking more like someone who was auditioning for the part of a bag lady than someone who was supposed to be a glamorous movie star. "Thea," she moaned, "do you have any aspirin?"

"Of course," Thea said. "Come upstairs and I'll get it for you."

As they left I sighed with relief. It really wasn't time to tell Thea yet.

I couldn't wait to test my new theory on the rest of the clues in this third group. When I re-read Laura's clue, I smothered a laugh. Laura had said something about a goose that laid a golden egg, and she was right. Augustus hadn't accused *Laura* of laying an egg. He'd been referring to the goose, and there was no doubt about it—a golden egg would certainly be a doozy.

I had the key to the third set of clues, and I was so excited, my fingers trembled.

I stopped making notes. Alex might come back, or someone else who'd feel he could just help himself to everything I'd worked out. In fact, this room was much too public to suit me. I grabbed my things and ran, taking the stairs two at a time and scrambling twice as fast as I passed the burial urn on the landing. Once inside my own room I turned on the light, then slammed and locked the door, collapsing against it and gulping for air.

As soon as I had caught my breath I sat on the bed, my back to the wall so I could keep watch on the door, and went through the third set of clues, one by one. Golden, gold, golden, gold.

"The bald eagle has many kin." Sure. Of course. One of the bald eagle's kin is the *golden* eagle.

That left Buck's clue. "Pappy" was a miner, a forty-niner, and what did the miners in 1849 look for? Gold!

That was it! I had it! I let out a yelp, then slapped a hand over my mouth, hoping no one had heard me. I'd solved two out of the four sets of clues, which proved to me that Aunt Thea had been wrong in suspecting that Augustus had planned to trick his guests. He really *had* worked out legitimate clues for them to solve.

Get busy, I told myself. It was time to tackle the fourth set of clues.

They proved to be a lot harder because I couldn't find anything that linked them together.

It was pitch-dark outside by this time, and my stomach

had begun to rumble up and down the scale with hunger. Sometimes it was difficult for me to understand myself. I was in the house with a dead body, a murderer, and a ghost, and I was hungry?

No matter what the circumstances, I guess some things never change. It had been a long time since lunch, and I hoped that Tomás was working hard on dinner. Maybe, I thought, I should go downstairs before someone had to come all the way to the tower to call me.

I took one last look at the clues and for some reason began to read them aloud: " 'More silent than the tombs are' . . . 'Like Davy Jones's locker—minus the sea' . . . 'Deader than a doornail, green as a pea' . . . 'Tea and sympathy—done to death.' "

The strange feeling came back and began to grow—tingling through my body like a jolt of electricity—until all of a sudden the whole thing made sense!

In reading the clues aloud I heard a letter instead of a word in each sentence. "More silent than the tombs *R*" . . . "Like Davy Jones's locker—minus the *C*" . . .

Aunt Thea's clue was the only one without a letter sound, so I ignored it and wrote the letters next to each of the other sentences. I came up with RCPTY, which didn't make sense in itself, but I suspected it was a word with scrambled letters. No vowel, but a *Y* could substitute. TRYCP . . . PYRCT . . . CRYPT.

Crypt! Oh, my gosh! I was so excited, I bounced up and down, shaking and creaking the bed.

King's Golden Crypt. But where? Where?

A sudden thought stopped me in midbounce. How did Thea's clue work into all this: GIVE UP THE GHOST?

The last part of the clue fell into place as easily as

though someone had whispered the answer in my ear, and I knew! I knew! I knew where the manuscript was hidden!

It should have been obvious from the beginning that only an important official, a ruler, maybe a king, would be buried in a golden crypt! The crypt had to be the golden burial urn with the *ghost* in it!

The knock on my door was so sudden that I lost my balance and rolled off the bed, managing to bang my knee and break a fingernail.

"Dinner is served, Miss Burns," I heard Walter call. There was a pause before he asked, "Are you all right?"

I stuck my head out from under the bed and yelled back, "I'm fine, thank you."

"I thought I heard a . . . a thump."

How could I explain. "You did," I shouted at Walter. "I broke a fingernail. And then I bumped my . . . Oh, well . . . what I mean is . . ." I took a deep breath and calmly said, "I'll be down in a minute."

There was a pause, and I knew he had to be thinking what a dork I was, but he answered, "Very well, Miss Burns," and I could hear his footsteps softly descending the short flight of stairs.

My mind raced as I filed down the rough edge of my fingernail. What was I going to do with my notes? I couldn't leave them in my room. Someone had searched it before and might again. I couldn't even tear the sheets up and put them in a wastepaper basket somewhere, because anyone could come across the pieces and fit them together.

There was only one place I was pretty sure they'd be

safe. I folded the pages up into a tight square and stuffed them into my bra.

It took just a quick glance in the mirror to see that people might wonder why I'd suddenly become lopsided, so I removed the wad, divided it into two wads, and tucked them into both sides of my bra. Good. I protruded a little more than usual, but I didn't think anyone would notice.

But what was I going to do about the expression on my face? I looked as though I'd just discovered America. Or won a lottery. Or got picked for a quiz show.

While I tugged off my jeans and T-shirt and pulled a dress over my head, I practiced making bland, unemotional faces in the mirror. It didn't work.

I could wait until Walter came back to see what happened to me and tell him I was sick, but then I'd miss dinner. At the very thought of going hungry my stomach growled. No. I'd have to go downstairs and tough it out.

As I arrived the group was moving from the parlor toward the dining room, cocktail glasses still in hand. I slipped in between Thea and Laura and tried to look inconspicuous, which was hard to do with my door key and necklace every now and then swinging against the paper in my bra, making a sharp, slapping noise.

Thea and Laura looked at me questioningly, but I just drooped along, trying to keep my eyes on the floor.

"Samantha, are you feeling well?" Thea asked, and I could hear the concern in her voice. I felt guilty at being even the least little bit suspicious of Aunt Thea.

"I guess I'm tired," I answered. Tired. That was a good direction to take. My shoulders slumped, and I dropped into the first chair I came to.

"You've been working too hard trying to solve those horrible clues," Laura said.

The clues! Yes! Bursting with excitement, I almost bounced in my chair, but I was so terrified at giving myself away that I hunched my shoulders and kept my eyes on my plate, which, unfortunately, was still empty.

Thea felt my forehead. "You aren't running a fever," she said. "Maybe a little food will give you an energy boost."

I hoped it would be a lot of food. We started with a Caesar salad, which was a good omen, because at last we were eating something I knew about. I could hardly wait until everyone had been served and Thea raised her fork, but I didn't get a chance to begin eating, because I had to answer questions.

Buck's came first. "Have you got to first base with those clues, Sam?"

"They're tough," I mumbled.

"You made a start, though," Alex said, and again his gaze was penetrating. "As I remember, you wrote down 'Kings' for the solution to the first clues."

"Oh?" Julia asked, and everyone stopped eating to stare at me.

"*Second* clues," I said, wishing they'd leave me alone. "And the king wasn't a solution. It was only my guess." I took a long breath, and calmly added, in a burst of inspiration, "Senator Maggio said I was wrong and the key was the ace."

"That's correct," the senator affirmed. "The ace is always the top card."

"But what does it mean?" Laura asked.

Alex's eyes narrowed. "Ask Samantha," he said. "I think she knows."

I wished he'd stop staring at me like that. Deliberately and slowly I ate a bite of salad. It was delicious, so I took another bite.

"Well?" Alex asked again.

I looked up to see all of them still watching me, and again excitement bubbled up inside me like a soft drink coming out of a can right after you shake it. *I know, but I'm not going to tell you!* I thought, then quickly realized that my facial expression was going to give everything away.

I could see suspicion beginning to cloud Julia's face, and Senator Maggio and Buck glanced at each other. Alex smirked. Had I given away my secret? Suddenly I was frightened.

"What?" Laura asked, holding her hands palms up and staring from face to face. "What's the matter? Julia, why are you looking like that?"

I pulled a Laura trick. It was the only way I could think of to get out of this mess. I closed my eyes, covered my face with my hands, and cried, "You're asking too much of me!"

Immediately Aunt Thea's arms went around my shoulders, and she gently scolded the others. "We are the ones who were supposed to solve the clues and find the treasure. Samantha offered to help, and instead of thanking her, you're browbeating her. Can't you see how tired she is?"

"I'm sorry, Sam," Laura said.

I sat up, patting Thea's hand and nodding to Laura. "Thank you," I murmured. I was glad to get out of that tight spot and extra glad that Walter, who had busied himself at the table, hadn't removed my salad.

We ate in silence for a few minutes, but finally Thea put

down her fork and said, "I think we have to face facts. I felt from the beginning that the game Augustus was playing was that of cat and mouse and not the game he outlined to you. You've seen all the clues. The first set was threats. The rest are impossible. No one could solve them."

"Then why would he go to all that trouble?" Julia asked.

"Just to watch us squirm, to watch us try and fail," Thea said.

"Was he really that cruel?" Senator Maggio asked.

"I'm afraid you know the answer to that question," Thea said.

Her eyes became blurry with tears, and as they spilled over her cheeks I leaned toward her. "Aunt Thea," I begged, "don't cry. I'll tell—"

"Excuse me, Miss Burns," Walter said as I collided with his outstretched arm. I jumped back, and he added, "May I remove your salad plate?"

I nodded and leaned back.

"But what about the manuscript? What about the material Trevor wrote that threatens us?" Senator Maggio was so intent on the situation, he hadn't heard me. I glanced around the table, but no one was looking in my direction. They were as upset about what Augustus had written as the senator was.

I'd been about to tell everything to Aunt Thea—and to the others. *Stay cool*, I reminded myself again. I had to get my hands on that manuscript before the others found it and destroyed it.

I kept my peace during the rest of the meal, which wasn't hard because the suspects had so much they wanted to talk about: Had Augustus actually included their secrets in his manuscript, or had he been bluffing? It was obvious that he had come into possession of some facts, but just how far had he gone in repeating them? Would the manuscript contain only simple hints and allusions or would it spell out the stories in detail?

They complained about hunting for the manuscript copy in every place imaginable. Had this been a complete waste of time? Did a copy of the manuscript even exist? I concentrated on eating a breaded ham and chicken roll, but I listened to every word.

As chocolate fudge cake was served, Senator Maggio said, "I think we can relax and forget the whole thing. I am of the opinion that *if* a copy of the manuscript still exists, it is probably hidden away so carefully that it may never show up."

Laura spoke up hesitantly. "When the police come, they'll search the house. They're better at searching than we are. They'll find the manuscript. I know they will."

Julia groaned and said, "I hate to admit it, but Laura is right."

"What if none of us mentions the manuscript?" Alex suggested. "The police need never know."

"Trevor's computer file was wiped out, and his papers and disks were burned," the senator said, and looked down his nose at Alex with contempt. "They'll have to be told about the manuscript and Trevor's reason for inviting us here. Lying won't help."

Alex didn't flinch. "It wouldn't be lying. It would be avoiding the issue, just as *you* intend to do if we find the manuscript and destroy it."

"That's different."

"How?"

"I suggest," Thea broke in, "that we conduct another detailed search of Augustus's office. There are manuscript boxes in his files, and on the shelves in the office closet are countless boxes with content labels pasted on. No matter what the boxes are labeled, we'll open them and examine everything that's inside."

Finding that Augustus was well organized blew my theory. I had just about convinced Mom that I couldn't keep my room cleaned up because I was going to be a writer, and creative people were not as organized as other people. It just wasn't in their nature to worry about mundane things.

In our search we soon found that if a box was labeled *Correspondence with* The New York Times, that's exactly what it contained. *File folders* was filled with file folders, and *Clippings, Paris, 1962* was filled with newspaper articles from Paris newspapers.

No manuscript.

All that work with no result discouraged the others, but it just made me more impatient. Except for that one slip in which the look on my face might have given me away, I'd managed to cover what I'd learned, and I had actually been able to keep from running off at the mouth. Even more important than that, I'd been able to solve the clues.

I felt kind of proud of myself until I remembered that somehow, during the night so that no one would know, I had to sneak down a dark hallway and remove Augustus Trevor's manuscript from a haunted burial urn!

THIRTEEN

We drifted into the parlor. None of us were comfortable about being together, yet at the same time we didn't want to be apart. I was doing my best to build my courage so that later I could do what I needed to do, and at the moment I didn't have enough nerve to go into that dark upstairs hallway all by myself.

Laura groaned and draped herself across one of the sofas, complaining, "When is this horrible rain going to end!"

Thea answered, "Mrs. Engstrom told me that according to the latest radio weather news the storm has begun drifting north and west and should end tomorrow."

"Which means that your telephone service will resume," Senator Maggio said.

The room was silent as we held our breaths.

"Why, yes," Thea said. "The telephone company will probably be able to make repairs early in the day."

"Then we can put all this behind us!" Julia said.

Alex's lips stretched in that horrible fake smile, and he said, "On the contrary, Julia dear. Remember that a man has been murdered and we're all suspects. The police are going to want to know who committed the crime."

"And they'll search for the manuscript," Laura whispered. "They're going to find it. I know they are."

"There's nowhere left to search," Julia said.

"We have the clues Augustus gave us," Alex said. He turned that smile on me.

"I'm not going to do any more work on the clues," I told him, and met his gaze without backing down. Darlene would have been proud of me.

Mrs. Engstrom came into the room with a tray filled with delicate demitasse cups and a large silver pot of coffee. Silently, she began filling some of the cups and offering them to the guests.

Alex ignored her and kept after me. "Maybe you don't need to work on the clues any longer, Samantha, because you've already figured out the solution. Is that it?"

Senator Maggio slapped his cup on the table so hard that it rattled in its saucer. "I don't want to hear any more about those so-called clues!" he stated. "We have established that they were false and therefore of no value."

"You may have taken it upon yourself to assume that," Alex told him, "but there's no reason why the rest of us have to go along with you."

"Please, please, please don't argue!" Laura begged. "We're in enough trouble. We don't need any more bad things to happen."

At that moment the lights went out.

Laura shrieked, and Buck yelled, "Who did that? What happened?"

With no moonlight or starlight seeping through the heavy cloud cover, the room was completely dark. It was like being swallowed by a large, warm mouth, and I struggled to adjust my eyes, trying to make out shapes or shadows.

Thea spoke from somewhere in the blackness. "The generator's gone out, I'm afraid. We've had trouble with it before when there's been a great deal of wind with the rain. Seepage into the motor, or some problem like that. I don't remember exactly what Augustus said about it."

"Can it be fixed?" Buck asked.

"Oh, yes. Chuck—you met him—he pilots our launch and is our general handyman, and he's very good with the generator. The only problem is that Chuck is on the mainland."

In the distance I saw a pinprick of light. It wavered and shivered and grew in size as it came closer and closer. I tried to yell a warning, but my throat froze and my tongue turned to ice. All that came out was a gargling gulp.

It was just as well I hadn't screamed, because the light turned out to be a candle carried by Mrs. Engstrom. She'd brought a basket of candles and candle holders, and as soon as all the candles had been lit the room looked soft and pretty, as though we'd been having a party instead of scaring ourselves to death.

"With the generator out of service, we won't have heat, so I've sent Walter and Lucy to put extra blankets in all the rooms," Mrs. Engstrom said. "We have a few flashlights in the bottom of the basket for those who want them, and if there is anything at all we can do to make you more comfortable, please don't hesitate to ask."

I liked the idea of a flashlight. It seemed much more

reliable than a candle, so I helped myself to one of the flashlights as well as a candle, kissed Aunt Thea good night, and went upstairs. I had a lot more courage now that I knew Lucy and Walter were upstairs too.

I paused on the landing. The light from my candle touched the carvings on the burial urn, and they winked and flickered like tiny, evil eyes. It would be so easy to grab the manuscript now and run with it to my tower room.

But as I hesitated a voice spoke above me on the stairs. Lucy said, as she came toward me, "I put two extra blankets on your bed, Miss Burns, because that tower room is little with lots of windows and can get awfully cold."

"Thanks," I said.

She stood on the landing with me, so there wasn't anything else to do but climb the stairs and head for my room.

"Good luck," Lucy whispered.

I turned and gave her a quick nod of gratitude. I needed all the good luck I could get.

Once I was in my room I blew out my candle. I wrapped myself in one of the extra blankets and sat halfway down the narrow stairs, leaving the door to the hallway open just a crack. I heard snatches of conversation, a couple of "good nights," and doors closing as the others straggled up to bed. I wished I'd thought of counting the closing of doors. Had everyone gone to bed? Was it safe now to go after the manuscript?

Too scared to do anything else, I waited for a while, then finally got enough nerve to creep down the last few tower stairs and enter the hallway. Although I had the flashlight in hand, I couldn't turn it on. Someone might see the light. So I moved to the left side of the hall, feeling my way along the wall through the blackness. Twice I stopped, listening intently. Had I heard a noise nearby or was my imagination working overtime?

Carefully, one hand sliding against the wall, I moved forward step by step. I had almost reached the top of the stairs when my fingers bumped into something hard and warm, something that jerked away, moving fast.

Before I could do more than gasp, an arm wrapped itself around my shoulders, and a hand pressed against my mouth.

I tried to yell, but Alex said, "Be quiet, Sam." He took the flashlight out of my hand and released me.

I jerked away and brushed myself off, wishing I could see him face-to-face. "What do you think you're doing?" I demanded.

"Keeping guard," he said.

"Guard against what?"

"Against you," he answered. I couldn't see his smile, but I could hear the mockery in his voice.

"Why? What did you expect me to do? Rob you while you slept?" I wished I had bitten his hand while it was against my mouth.

"I think you know where the manuscript is," Alex said.

"Don't be silly." I could hear the quaver in my own voice and regretted not sounding more positive.

"You know where it is and were going to get it."

A door opened, and candlelight flickered into the hallway. "Is something the matter?" Aunt Thea asked.

Smooth as a snake slipping into a hole, Alex answered, "Samantha and I were headed in the same direction—down to the kitchen."

"Oh, dear," Thea said, "you're hungry. The electric

stove won't work, of course, so a hot cup of coffee or tea is out of the question, but there's sure to be cold meat and cheeses, and we can make sandwiches." She tied the belt on the robe she'd been clutching together and stepped into the hallway. "I'll go with you."

"There's no need," Alex said. "We can find everything ourselves."

"Why don't you come, Aunt Thea?" I asked. "You might be hungry too."

She rested a hand on my shoulder. "I can't sleep," she said, "so a visit to the kitchen sounds like a good idea."

Alex turned away, but I had seen the angry frustration on his face. *Too bad for you*, I thought.

Another door opened, and Julia stepped out, carrying a candle. Her robe was neatly tied, and her hair was freshly brushed. "I hope you don't mind my overhearing the last part of your conversation," she said. "I'm going downstairs with you."

"Come along." Thea smiled. "We'll make a nice party out of it."

We walked down to the landing. I kept my eyes away from the burial urn by sticking close to the banister, but that was a mistake, because as I leaned over, looking down into the entry hall, I caught the gleam in eyes that were staring back at me. I started and clutched the banister, but it was only Mrs. Engstrom.

She was still fully dressed, and I wondered why. Had she stationed herself in the entry hall to keep guard, just as Alex had stationed himself in the upstairs hallway? Alex had been waiting to see if I'd make a move, but why was Mrs. Engstrom on watch? Was she protecting Thea?

She met us at the foot of the stairs and led the way

toward the kitchen. "Would you like some wine with your sandwiches?" she asked Thea. "I'll be happy to get it for you. Red? A nice Merlot?"

She opened a door which led to some steep stone stairs, and I said, "I'll get the wine for you, Mrs. Engstrom." I snatched my flashlight out of Alex's hand before he was aware of what I was doing, and began descending the stairs—thirteen of them. I counted.

"The Merlot is on the right, near the door," Mrs. Engstrom called, then added, "It's very nice of you to do this, Miss Burns."

I felt guilty about getting credit for being nice when my real reason for offering to get the wine was to see that wine cellar, which had the only door in the house that could be locked to stay locked. An idea was beginning to grow in my mind. The key was in the door, and it turned easily.

I swept the small room with my beam of light, touching row after row of bottles lying on their sides. I could see footprints smudging other footprints all over the dusty floor. Some of the prints must have been made by Walter when he came for wine, and some were made by Julia and Alex and whoever else might have searched this room for the manuscript. It didn't take long to find a couple of bottles of Merlot. I blew some dust off the bottles and carried them back upstairs.

By this time I was shaking. The house was chilly, but the wine cellar was really cold. As I entered the kitchen I shoved the bottles at Alex, who had to take them or lose them, and said, "I'm freezing! I'm going to run upstairs and get my blanket. I'll be right back."

Alex didn't have time to object, and I was pretty sure

that with Thea there he wouldn't run after me. I scrambled up the main stairs to the landing, swooped the beam of the flashlight in a quick arc to make sure no one was around, and turned it off. Tucking the flashlight under my chin I rested my left hand on the urn to balance it and lifted the lid with my right.

A soft hiss seemed to come from the unsealed urn as warm, stale air swept over my hand like crawly fingers.

I squeezed my eyes tightly shut and tried to keep my teeth from chattering as I whispered, "Listen to me, O Honorable Royal Ghost Person. I'm not your enemy. I'm your friend. I'm sorry if somebody got careless with your ashes along the way. I can't do anything about that, but I can remove the manuscript that's stuffed right down your middle so you can rest undisturbed. Okay?"

I didn't wait for an answer. I really didn't want one. If a voice had come out of that urn, I probably would have dropped dead on the spot. Slowly, carefully, I reached down into the urn until my fingers touched something hard. As I explored the object I knew I'd been right. Hidden inside this urn was Augustus Trevor's manuscript!

I grabbed the tightly rolled sheets of paper, which were fastened with rubber bands, took a firm grip, and pulled. The roll was thick and heavy, but I got it out and tucked it under one arm. As I replaced the lid on the urn, I remembered to whisper "thank you" before I ran down the hallway to my room.

All I wanted to do was read that manuscript, but I couldn't. I had to go back to the kitchen or Alex would know something was wrong. So I stuffed the manuscript inside the pillowcase, straightened the bed, wrapped one of the extra blankets around my shaking self—by this time

I had more than one reason to shake—and hurried downstairs, using the flashlight as a guide.

Alex looked up with surprise as I returned, but Thea and Julia were well into a lively discussion of modern theater as they busied themselves by putting together a half-dozen or so sandwiches, so they paid no attention to me. I huddled into one of the chairs, bent almost double, and continued to shake, tremble, and shiver like a poor pitiful thing beyond hope.

Thea glanced in my direction and broke off in midsentence. "Samantha!" she cried. "Are you ill?"

"I don't know," I said. "I'm cold, right down to my bones."

"You're having chills," she said, and came around the table toward me.

Thea's hand on my forehead was cool and comfortable, so I said what I knew she'd come out with. "I don't have a fever. I'm just cold. That's all."

"Maybe a little food . . ."

"I'm not hungry. I'm cold, and I'm tired. I just want to go to bed."

"That's probably a good idea," Thea said. "I'd suggest that you sleep in your clothes. Wrap up in one of the blankets before you get under the covers. Within a few minutes your body heat should make the bed nice and toasty."

"I'll try it," I said, and stood up, clutching the blanket tightly around my shoulders.

Alex got to his feet and yawned. "I'm tired, too, Thea. I'll see you in the morning."

"What about all these sandwiches?" Julia asked. "I thought you wanted to eat some of them."

"Save them until tomorrow," Alex said.

I left the room with Alex right behind me. Neither of us spoke to the other until we arrived at the door to the stairs that led to my tower room.

I stopped and glared at him. "Where do you think you're going?"

He grinned nastily. "I'm going to close the door at the foot of your stairs and sit with my back against it. You won't be able to leave your room to get the manuscript, because I'll be right here to stop you." He paused, one eyebrow wiggling upward. "Of course, you can always take me with you to get the manuscript."

"I hope you're comfortable sitting out here in the cold," I told him, "because I'm going to bed. I'm not going hunting for a manuscript."

He smiled again. "I'll make sure of that."

I shut the door at the bottom of my curved flight of stairs and heard him settle against it. It was all I could do to keep from laughing as I hurried up the stairs, shut and locked my bedroom door, and pushed the little chair against it, wedging it tightly under the knob.

So far, so good, I thought. I removed Augustus's manuscript from the pillowcase and propped myself against the headboard, the blanket around me, the covers pulled up high. Then—so excited that my breath came in bursts and gulps—I removed the rubber bands that kept the manuscript rolled, spread it out on my lap, and trained the flashlight on the title page.

FOURTEEN

"*Tarnished Gold*, by Augustus Trevor," I whispered aloud to myself, then began to skim through the pages.

There was some fascinating stuff in that manuscript, a lot of it about famous people I'd heard of. I would have loved to read the whole thing, because right away I saw that this was full of secret behind-the-scenes stories I couldn't wait to tell Darlene; but there were four hundred and eighty-two pages in this manuscript, and I didn't have enough time. According to my watch, it was close to one in the morning.

I searched each page for the names of the people Augustus had invited to play his horrible game, but it wasn't until I reached page 105 that I found the first name: Laura Reed. Augustus wrote well, and that was the problem. He drew me right into Laura's story, and I could see this young Hollywood actress who had made a good start and had a promising career to look forward to. But she had a problem that could cause all her dreams to vanish: an equally young husband named Larry, who was jealous of his wife and her new life that excluded him. After an argument in which Larry had insisted she forget Hollywood, Laura had tried to patch things up. The use of a sailboat, offered by a director friend . . . a day on the ocean . . . It should have been idyllic, but late that afternoon a hysterical Laura had brought the boat back alone. According to her story, as they'd turned the boat toward shore Larry had been hit by the swinging boom and knocked overboard. Laura claimed to have searched for him until finally, in desperation, she gave up and returned to the dock. Two days later, Larry's body washed ashore at Emerald Bay.

His death was ruled an accident, but many years later Augustus discovered that the boat had *not* been offered by that director friend. Laura had asked for its use. And it wasn't until later that the owner had noticed that a mallet, which was part of the ship's equipment, was missing. He'd thought nothing of it, deciding it had been misplaced, but Augustus had drawn a different conclusion.

I put down the manuscript, shocked by what I'd read. Augustus had practically called Laura a murderer! Maybe she'd been telling the truth. Then again, maybe she hadn't. If she'd murdered one person who had got in her way, she could have murdered Augustus, as well.

This was heavy stuff to think about, and it scared me, but I thumbed through a few more pages and came to Alex Chambers's name.

I already knew that Alex was a stinker, but I didn't know how truly rotten he was until I read what Augustus had to say about him. Alex Chambers, the famous dress designer, had made investments under a fake corporation name, and these investments consisted of New York sweatshops, staffed by recent immigrants, many of them children, most of them people from Vietnam who couldn't speak English.

I'd seen a television exposé of sweatshops, so I knew exactly what Augustus was writing about: guards and padlocked gates at the doors while people bent over sewing machines ten to twelve hours a day for very low pay. Alex Chambers, who publicly gave generous amounts to charity at balls where the women wore his expensive creations—just how wonderful would they think he was if they knew how much of his income came from badly mistreating workers, many of them children?

Would Alex have killed Augustus to keep his secret from being exposed? It was possible.

Fifty pages on I found Augustus's story about Buck Thompson. In 1979, the last year Buck had played pro ball, he'd fumbled the ball at a crucial time in a big game, and his team had won by a close two points. Buck had claimed a back injury, even spending two weeks in the hospital, but Augustus had come up with an informant, a bookie named Willie Peeples, who'd sworn that Buck had secretly bet on the point spread for this game and other games, and in his manuscript Augustus accused Buck of faking his injury in order to control the score.

I winced, thinking about Buck's commercials and work with kids. What would happen to this well-known role model if Augustus's information was printed? To keep the story from being made public, could Buck have killed Augustus? Buck was strong, and he had quite a temper.

Groaning, hating what I had to do, I kept turning pages until I got to Senator Arthur Maggio. A number of years ago his son had been an attorney for one of the organized crime families—Bonino. So that's where I had heard the name! But the senator's son had gone into corporate law, breaking any ties with the Boninos, and the Maggios claimed to be free from that taint.

But not according to Augustus, who insisted that no one ever leaves the mob. Augustus suggested that the generous funds raised and donated by some of the senator's Political Action Committees had come straight from the Boninos, and wouldn't the crime families love to have a president of the United States in their pocket!

I'd overheard my parents talking about Senator Maggio and how he'd spent most of his life working toward his goal of being elected president. Even though we weren't that close to the presidential primaries, his campaign was already under way. The senator couldn't afford to let Augustus publish that information. So what had he done about it?

My jaw actually dropped open, like in a cartoon, when I read what Augustus had to say about Julia. I'd been told about her good friend who destroyed all her manuscripts and killed herself, but according to what Augustus had discovered, after piecing together information from "reliable sources," that wasn't the way it happened. The manuscripts had been secretly carted off by Julia and her husband, Jake, who had been with her friend at the time she jumped. Jumped or was pushed—who was to say?

It wasn't a simple matter of Julia sending the manuscripts out under her name instead of her friend's name. Julia's husband, as co-conspirator, got into the act first, spicing up the plots with graphic scenes, adding the steamy "Julia Bryant" touches that had made Julia famous. Julia was nothing but a front for the novels!

No wonder Julia didn't remember her own characters. They belonged to her once best friend who'd grown up with her in Buffalo.

Maybe it was staying up so late without sleep, maybe it was the fear that came from being trapped in a house with a killer, or maybe it was the awful feeling of being a spy in other people's lives, but I felt terrible. I hugged the rest of the manuscript to my chest, pulled up my knees and rested my forehead against them.

Augustus must have had enough proof that the stories he wrote about took place, or he would have been sued for writing such things. The people he wrote about weren't likely to be arrested, but they still had something to be afraid of, an urgent reason that the stories shouldn't be published. All of them were dependent on public approval, and without it their careers were down the drain.

If Augustus's information was right, then two of them —Julia and Laura—had already committed murder.

Well, that was that. I hadn't learned a thing except information I really didn't want to know. Any one of the five suspects could have murdered Augustus.

Five? Oh, oh, I'd forgotten Aunt Thea.

I searched the rest of the manuscript, and it wasn't until page 356 that I discovered Thea's story.

In 1962, she and Augustus had rented a private villa in Acapulco, taking with them only Mrs. Engstrom, who—as usual when they traveled—took charge of domestic matters and hired local people to staff the house.

One day Thea went alone to shop in town. Thinking she knew the way, she cut through a back alley to reach a shop on another street. She'd been followed by someone who came up behind her, slashing at the straps of her handbag with a knife. Thea had resisted and in the struggle had fallen, dragging the robber down with her. Thea had managed to stagger to her feet, but the robber lay facedown in the dirt without moving. Thea had grabbed his shoulders, turned him over, and saw the knife protruding from his chest. She also saw he was only a boy.

Terrified, knowing that she could be arrested for murder, Thea ran from the empty alley, caught a taxi, and returned to the villa, where she made the mistake of telling her husband what had happened.

Why had Augustus threatened Thea with this story now—after all this time? Had he really intended to use it in his book? Or was he just trying to make her suffer?

Thea had killed, I told myself, but I quickly answered back, *No! Not Aunt Thea. The death was an accident. She'd never commit murder.*

At that moment the light tap at my door and the whisper of my name were more terrifying than if someone had broken down the door.

"Who's there? Who are you?" I shouted. I threw off my blankets and leaped from the bed. The manuscript pages went flying.

"Samantha dear. It's me—Thea. Will you open the door, please?"

"Yes," I answered. "Right away." I swooped up loose pages and stuffed them together, not caring about the order. Did I have them all? Yes. Thank goodness. But where to put them?

"Samantha?" Thea asked.

I quickly stuffed the manuscript under the mattress at

the head of the bed and stumbled to the door, tugging away the chair and turning the key.

As Thea entered the room she gave me a curious look and again rested a hand on my forehead. "Dear me, it *is* cold up here," she said. "Maybe you'd be more comfortable if you shared my room tonight."

"No, thank you," I said. I took a long, slow breath, gestured toward the chair, and said, "Please sit down, Aunt Thea." I was proud of myself. Just one day ago I would have been so nervous, I'd have given everything away, but through this weekend I'd learned a little game-playing of my own, and at the moment I was calm and cool and in charge of myself. I liked the feeling.

"When I found out what Alex was up to I sent him to his room, and I want to assure you he'll stay there," Thea said. "Such stupidity, sitting in the hallway, practically keeping you prisoner, just because he has the ridiculous idea that you know the location of the manuscript."

I quickly turned away so that she couldn't see my face and fell over the chair. So much for being in charge.

"Are you all right, dear?" Aunt Thea asked.

"I'm fine," I squeaked, although I really wasn't. From my hands-and-knees position I could see a page from Augustus's manuscript lying on the floor, half under the bed, half out. It was too far away for me to reach, and it was in plain view. What if Thea saw it?

Thea bent to lend me a hand and help me to my feet, and my mind raced, trying to come up with a way to cover that page without drawing attention to it.

Zilch. Zero. *Nada.* I was all out of good ideas.

FIFTEEN

Thea didn't sit down, and I didn't either. I kept myself between Thea and that sheet of paper. Surely, if she saw it she'd recognize the print and know immediately where it had come from.

"Have you been able to sleep, Samantha?" Thea asked.

"No," I said honestly, "but I'm tired now."

She smiled and slipped an arm around my shoulders. I kept edging sideways, trying to turn her back to the manuscript page. Thea looked a little puzzled, but she said, "I'm sorry your visit has turned out so badly, dear. I'd looked forward to it with so much pleasure."

"So had I," I mumbled. This was my mother's aunt, and I was treating her like one of the suspects. How could I? She had been married to Augustus and probably had inherited everything he owned. That included his manuscript, so she had a right to know that I'd found it. "Aunt Thea," I began.

But she ignored me, going on with what she had in mind. "Your mother told me that you were bringing some of your stories, hoping that Augustus would critique them for you. I'm sorry that has been a disappointment to you, as well. Unfortunately, Augustus wasn't generous with young writers, and he was not likely to have guided you, either. Your mother said that you felt unable to proceed with a writing career without guidance—"

"Aunt Thea," I interrupted, "there's something I want to tell you."

"Before you do," she said, "I'd like to point out that you must have dropped a page from one of your stories. It's there on the floor, and I know you don't want to lose it."

At that moment we heard a loud thud, a thumping, and a terrible crash.

Aunt Thea and I raced out of the room, down the stairs, and into the hallway, waving our flashlights ahead of us. The beams of light flew from ceiling to wall to floor like flashes of lightning, exposing Julia, Laura, and Senator Maggio, who came flying out of their rooms.

"What is it?"

"What's going on?"

The thumping continued, and we raced toward the source.

On the landing Buck gripped Alex by the shoulders, banging him up and down against the floor. Alex held the open burial urn in his right hand, and he bounced it with all his strength against Buck's broad back.

"Stop it!" Thea commanded. "Stop it this minute!"

There was so much anger and authority in her voice that the two men separated. They sat and stared upward. Alex's self-assuredness had vanished, and Buck pouted like a mad little kid.

"What's this all about?" Thea asked.

"I caught him in my room," Buck growled. "He ran, and I chased him."

Alex smiled as his poise began to return. "I thought Buck was asleep. It seemed like a good opportunity to look at the first clue Augustus had given him."

Buck muttered something, and for a moment I thought he was going to hit Alex, but Alex got to his feet and glanced in my direction. "I realized that Samantha was right. The clues we got weren't enough. If it would help to see the first clues . . . well, I'd just be a step ahead of the rest of you in finding out."

The others were all so angry they began yelling at Alex, but I kept thinking about His Royal Scariness and how furious he must be at the way his urn had been treated. Raising my voice so that it was even louder, I shouted at Alex, "What are you doing with that burial urn?"

Alex looked at the urn, which was still in his hand, shrugged, and placed it back on the pedestal, which wobbled a bit then settled itself. "I needed something to protect myself," he answered.

"You shouldn't have used that burial urn," I told him.

Alex picked up his flashlight and aimed it at me. "Why not? What's so special about this urn?" he asked, and said to the others, "Look at Samantha's face. She knows something."

I knew *everything*, and I couldn't let my face give me away. "I'll tell you what I know," I said. "According to Walter, the urn is haunted."

"I've had as much of this place as I can stand!" Laura wailed, and began to cry.

While they were busy trying to out-shout and out-argue each other, I ran down to the landing, picked up the lid to the burial urn, and replaced it. The urn felt warm to my touch, and I patted it gently. "You must know by this time that the world is full of weirdos," I whispered. "Sorry you had to run into a couple more of them."

In just a few hours it would be daylight and the telltale expression on my face would be easy for everyone to read. I had to distract them. I had to take their minds away from me. The clues . . . Alex had said the clues they had got weren't enough. Okay, I'd give them another set.

"Lend me a hand," I said to the urn, "and you'll soon be left in peace. I've got to get something. If any of them notices that I've gone, will you please distract them?" Oh, well, it couldn't hurt to ask.

I turned off my flashlight and felt my way down the rest of the stairs, across the entry hall, and along the way to Augustus's office. I entered the room and closed the door behind me before I turned on my flashlight.

It took only a few minutes to find envelopes and paper that matched those he'd used for the clues, but I had to scribble with half a dozen pens before I found the one with the bright blue ink. I tucked the pen in my jeans pocket and slipped the paper and envelopes inside the front of my shirt, next to my skin.

It wasn't hard to find my way in the dark going back. The sky had grown lighter, and there were even shadows cast by the moon. Thank goodness the storm was over!

As I neared the stairs I heard Thea ask, "Where's Samantha?"

At that moment there was a crash. Alex let out a yelp, and Buck shouted, "You pushed it! You tried to get me!"

"I did not!"

I took the stairs two at a time and shone my flashlight

beam on the urn, which lay on the floor, the toppled pedestal next to it.

"Yeah? How did that thing fall over if you didn't push it?"

I stooped and gently picked up the urn, straightening its lid and stroking its sides. "You probably knocked it off balance earlier while the two of you were fighting," I told Buck. "If you'll please pick it up, I'll put the urn where it belongs."

The pedestal was heavy, and it took both Buck and Alex to raise it. They tested, to make sure it was secure, before I returned the royal burial urn to its rightful place. "Thanks," I whispered to the urn.

"You're welcome," Alex said.

I stepped past him and said to Thea, "It isn't going to do any good to argue with Alex. I don't care what he does. I'm going to bed."

"Good idea," Julia said, but she glared at Alex. "Don't waste your time searching my room, because I didn't keep my first clue. I tore it into little pieces and flushed them away."

Laura gasped, and I could practically hear her mind begin to work. Her first clue would be the next to go.

"Back to bed, all of us," Thea said. She kissed my cheek, told me to sleep well, and I followed my flashlight beam up to the tower room, again barricading the door with the chair.

I would have loved to sleep, but there was something I had to do first. Just to be on the safe side I put the manuscript pages back in order, rolled them tightly, and fastened them with the rubber bands.

No one was in the hallway. I was pretty sure that none

of them would wander out of their rooms again, so I sneaked down to the landing and replaced the manuscript inside the urn.

"It's terrible to bother you again, Your Excellent Ghostliness, after all that you did for me, if that really was you," I whispered, "but I can't take any chances. The very minute the police arrive I'll take this thing out of your royal middle, and you'll be left in peace and quiet. Is that all right?"

I thought I detected a faint hum, and it didn't seem antagonistic, so I replaced the lid, ran back to my room, and barricaded the door again.

I was so exhausted, my head hurt and I went into a fit of yawning, but there was one last thing to do before I could sleep. I had to come up with clues that looked and sounded like the ones Augustus had invented so that they'd be accepted. But my clues had to have a single purpose—to lead all the suspects, except one, to the wine cellar.

You can do it, I told myself. *After all, you're a writer.*

If I hadn't been so tired, or if only Darlene had been with me, the job wouldn't have taken so long. On my legal pad I wrote, I crossed out, I wrote some more, and made dozens of changes until I had the clues the way I wanted them. Then neatly, trying to copy Augustus's printing, I wrote the clues, put them into the envelopes, and marked them all: *Game Clue* #5. To follow my plan I added, FINAL CLUE: WITH THIS ONE YOU'RE ON YOUR OWN.

I put the unsealed envelopes on the chest, rolled up in one of my blankets, the covers pulled up to my chin, and closed my eyes. Aunt Thea had been right. Even though the air in the room was freezing, my body heat began working, and soon even my toes were warm. I slept so hard, I didn't move until the sun woke me.

Sunlight! That meant the storm had passed and soon we'd be in touch with the rest of the world. Tag ends of clouds scraggled across an electric-blue sky, propelled by a wind that slapped at the treetops and churned flips of white foam across the top of the rough and choppy water.

I glanced at my watch, amazed to find it was already ten o'clock. I had planned on being downstairs first, and now maybe my plan wouldn't work, because the others were bound to be up. There was nothing else to do but give it my best shot, so I washed my face—there was only cold water—and dressed.

Lucy came from one of the bedrooms and joined me as I walked down the stairs. "Do you need anything?" she asked. "Better tell me now, because Walter, Tomás, and I have cleanup work to do in the other house. One part of the roof leaked badly."

"I don't need anything," I told Lucy. "I'm fine."

But I wasn't fine. I was scared. I had no idea if my plan would work.

I didn't hide the envelopes in my pocket. I carried them in my right hand, and as I entered the dining room, where Laura, Buck, Julia, and Alex were eating cold cereal and bananas, I held the envelopes high, waving them.

"Look what I found," I said. "The fifth set of game clues. They're the final ones too."

Alex leaned forward, studying my face. "What are you hiding?" he asked. "Your face gives you away. What do you know that we don't know?"

"All right!" I slammed the envelopes down on the table. "I read them. I know they have your names on them and they're supposed to be for your private information, but I read them anyway. Okay?"

"It's okay with me," Laura said. "Sam *is* supposed to be helping us."

"She hasn't been any help so far," Alex grumbled, but my embarrassment at being "caught" seemed to satisfy him.

Julia snatched up her envelope and stood, pushing back her chair. "Thea and Arthur are in the sun-room. I'll get them," Julia told us and hurried out of the room.

I'd been waiting for the big question, and as soon as we were all seated around the table, with Mrs. Engstrom bringing in refills of coffee, sugar, and cream, Alex asked it.

"Where did you find this set of clues, Samantha?"

I was prepared. "In one of Julia's books, her main character finds a packet of love letters hidden behind a bedroom mirror. Isn't that right, Julia?"

I paused and looked at Julia, who smiled, then nodded. Of course I'd made all that up, but she didn't know her own books, because they weren't her own books.

"So I looked behind the mirror in Augustus's room, and there was the packet of letters, tied with a rubber band and wedged behind the frame."

"Imagine! Just like in Julia's book!" Laura said.

Alex shrugged, which meant, I suppose, that he bought my story.

Buck scowled at the envelope in his hand. "What does this mean? 'Final Clue: With this one you're on your own'?" he asked.

"I assume that this was Trevor's attempt to separate the sheep from the goats," Senator Maggio said, and he didn't attempt to hide the sarcasm in his voice. "It's fairly obvious that once again we're on our own."

"Samantha read *all* the clues," Alex said. "Maybe we should ask her about them."

I didn't like the disappointed look Thea gave me, but when all of this was over I was sure she'd understand. I had started this, and I had to finish it. "This time it won't help you to share the clues," I said. "All I can tell you is that the clues lead to a place in the house you have to find and go to, and I don't think they'll be hard to figure out."

Laura leaned toward me. "Did you figure it out?"

I nodded.

"Tell us."

"Open your envelope. Look at your clue. You can work it out," I said.

She did, and stared at the words so hard, she squinted.

The others read their clues, and I watched their faces intently. Had I made the clues too hard? Too easy?

Five of the clues were the same: ONE ACROSS, THIRTEEN DOWN. WHO FINDS A MESSAGE IN A BOTTLE?

Alex studied his clue intently. All of a sudden his eyes widened and a puzzled expression spread across his face. He quickly glanced at the others, then slid back his chair, picking up the flashlight he'd brought down with him. He casually strolled out of the dining room in the direction of the wine cellar.

Julia murmured "Hmmm" a few times, then said, "Oh! But we . . ." As cautious as Alex had been, she quietly left, going the same way.

I was pretty sure they had guessed the answer I wanted them to come up with.

Thea got to her feet but hesitated. She gave me an odd

look, glanced at those who were left at the table, then walked through the door leading to the entry hall.

Mrs. Engstrom followed her, and that was fine with me.

Senator Maggio looked up from his sheet of paper, then down again, mumbling under his breath. "It must be," he said aloud. He pushed back his chair, snatched up the only flashlight that was left, and strode toward the door to the cellar stairs.

"The first part sounds like a crossword puzzle, but there's no puzzle here. I'll never figure it out!" Laura complained.

She probably wouldn't, and that could ruin everything, so I said, "Then why don't you follow Senator Maggio? He seems to know where he's going."

Laura and Buck scrambled to their feet and ran after the senator.

I followed at a more leisurely pace.

One across . . . the dining room. Thirteen down . . . the stone steps leading to the wine cellar. Five suspects were in the cellar now, probably searching for the manuscript in and among the rows of wine bottles.

They didn't even notice as I walked down the steps. I silently closed the door, locked it, and pocketed the key.

It was time now to join Thea. I'd sent her to the sunroom with the clue ON THE BEST OF DAYS THIS IS WHERE YOU'LL GET YOUR RAYS.

I knew it wasn't worded the way Augustus Trevor would have worded it. Thea had probably guessed that these were my clues and not her husband's, which was why she had given me that strange look. She'd want an explanation, but that was okay. I planned to tell Aunt Thea everything.

SIXTEEN

Just as I flopped into a wicker chair across from Aunt Thea, the phone jangled in my ear, startling me so much that I jumped to my feet and reached for it.

But Mrs. Engstrom was one step ahead of me. She picked up the receiver and listened a moment. "Thank you," she said formally, and hung up, turning to Thea. "The phone service has been restored, Mrs. Trevor."

"Mrs. Engstrom!" I interrupted. "You didn't tell them about the murder!"

"The caller was simply an employee of the telephone company," Mrs. Engstrom answered. "Besides, it is your aunt's prerogative to inform the police, not mine." She walked across the room and began to open the filmy curtains that shaded the windows. The room was bright with sunlight, but the trees outside the windows bent and shimmered in the wind.

"Aunt Thea?"

"Yes, I'll call them," Thea said, but she didn't move. I

could hear the exhaustion in her voice as she added, "I had so hoped that we'd find the manuscript in time."

I sat down and leaned toward her. "We did. I found it."

"You what?"

"I worked out the clues. They gave me the answer."

"Why didn't you tell me, Samantha?"

"Because it didn't seem like the right time until now."

"What does this particular time have to do with it?"

"Aunt Thea," I said, "your husband didn't make up the last set of clues. I did. I think you figured that out, but the others didn't."

"Yes. I wasn't sure what you were doing, Samantha, but I trusted you."

That made me feel awfully guilty, and I hurried to explain, "We don't have to worry about the suspects. They followed my clues to the wine cellar, and I locked them in."

Thea stared at me in amazement. "You didn't!"

"I had to. While they're down there we can talk about what Augustus wrote about them. Maybe together we can discover who committed the murder."

"You read the manuscript?"

"Parts of it. The parts about *them.*" My voice dropped to one notch above a whisper. "And about you." Quickly I briefed her on what Augustus had written about each of the suspects.

Tears came to Thea's eyes, and she said, "I don't understand why you weren't open with me right from the beginning." She stood up and reached for my hands, pulling me out of my chair. "Come with me, Samantha. Show me where the manuscript is hidden."

"It's right where Augustus hid it, in that golden burial

urn on the landing." I balked, tugging at her hands. "Aunt Thea, please call the police right away. They'll know how much time went by between the time you found out your phone was working and the time you made the call. If you wait too long it will look suspicious."

Thea thought about this for only an instant. She gave a brisk nod, picked up the phone, and called the police. The conversation was brief, and after she hung up she told me, "They said the sea is still quite rough so they'll have to use one of their cruisers. It will take them close to an hour to get here."

"Then we've got time to talk and try to work this out," I said. "Please, Aunt Thea. I told you where the manuscript is, and you know that no one can get to it except you. Please help me find out who committed the murder."

"Half an hour," Thea said. "That's all." She allowed me to lead her to the nearest sofa and sat down beside me. "Where do we start?"

"Which one of the suspects had the strongest reason for murdering Augustus?"

She shook her head. "According to what you told me they each had a reason. I think it all comes down to personality. Which one would be most inclined to commit murder?"

"I don't think Laura could do it."

"No, and no matter what Augustus claimed about the death of Laura's first husband, there wouldn't be enough substantial proof to make a case. Would scandal hurt her? I don't think so. The publicity might even help her career."

"So Laura's out. What about Julia?"

"If Augustus didn't have solid proof about the death of Julia's friend, it adds up to nothing more than rumor."

"What about leaking the information that Julia doesn't write her own books? That could be damaging, couldn't it?"

Thea sighed. "The people who read the kind of novels Julia writes might be a little shocked at discovering she's simply a figurehead, but I doubt if she'd lose many readers. It's the sensationalism they're interested in, not the author."

"We're making progress. We've already wiped out two suspects," I said, excited by what we were accomplishing. I began to feel like a detective character in a mystery novel. "How about Alex Chambers and the sweatshops he makes a profit from?"

"The city officials have to know about the existence of the sweatshops," Thea told me. "The shops were even the subject of one of the national television news magazines. If the authorities want to make arrests, they can."

"But what about Alex's reputation?"

"If his customers cared more about his treatment of people than about his latest creations . . ." The corners of her mouth turned down and she shook her head. "I'm afraid only a few of them might."

My excitement was giving way to discouragement. "Senator Maggio?" I asked.

Thea sighed. "Don't you think that if Augustus could come up with information about Arthur's ties to organized crime, then some sharp reporters and politicians from the other party could too? Probably they're waiting with the information until Arthur announces his candidacy. Arthur knows this. He's too intelligent to commit murder."

"That leaves Buck," I said.

"I don't know what the statute of limitations is on the crime Buck committed, but he's been out of pro football for years. His reputation would suffer, but would it matter so much to Buck that he'd commit murder?"

"Buck has a bad temper."

"A bad temper isn't necessarily a prerequisite for committing murder. Hate . . . fear . . . there are other factors to take into consideration."

"I can see why Augustus was willing to take out the stories about anyone who was able to solve his clues." I groaned and said, "Aunt Thea, this won't work. With your system we've eliminated all of the suspects."

"What about me, Samantha?" Thea asked quietly. "I'm a suspect too."

"No, you're not," I said. "You're my aunt, and anyway, what happened in Acapulco took place a long time ago. I know there isn't a statute of limitations on murder, but probably no one in Mexico even remembers the case or has any records on it."

"We can't be sure," Mrs. Engstrom said from the doorway.

Aunt Thea looked into my eyes. She seemed even more softly gray than ever, and she kind of folded into herself as she said, "I didn't kill Augustus, Samantha."

I squeezed her hands reassuringly. "I know you didn't. Let's look at this another way. Whoever killed Augustus knew something about computers, because the entire document file was erased."

Thea said, "If you remember, everyone claimed not to

understand computers. It seems as though I'm the only one in the group who knew how to use Augustus's computer."

Computer, I thought. *Computer*. It should mean something. I got a funny, tickling feeling in my mind, but I couldn't grasp it.

"Some of them lied," I said bluntly. "Senator Maggio knew how to turn on Augustus's computer. He even brought a lap-top with him. And Alex understands all about files and disks. Before dinner on Friday he was talking about computerizing his designs. Julia knows computers too, no matter what she claims."

Thea's fingers trembled. "How can we possibly accuse them of lying?"

"Maybe we won't have to. There's something else to go on. The person who killed Augustus didn't know how writers work—that there would be an extra copy of the manuscript. That might be the key."

Key? The moment I said the word, things began to fall into place.

Thea didn't answer. I could tell that she was thinking as hard as I was.

I clutched her hand more tightly now, this time because I was scared and I needed someone to cling to. "Your guests don't know that all the bedroom keys are the same and fit all the upstairs locks, do they?"

"Why, no," Thea said.

"Someone who did know about the keys searched my room, looking for the clue Augustus had given me—the one he lied about when he said it told more than all the others."

"Samantha, believe me. I didn't."

"I know that," I said, "because I know who did."

I twisted around and looked at Mrs. Engstrom, who was standing just inside the doorway, the rolled manuscript in her hands. "*You* knew about the keys, and you use a computer, so you know how they work."

Aunt Thea gripped my fingers so tightly, they hurt. She knew what was coming. "You'd do anything for my aunt, wouldn't you, Mrs. Engstrom?" I asked.

"Yes," she said. "I would." She crossed the room and stood in front of Thea. "When I saw that folder from Acapulco in your hands I knew what that horrible man had done. If his manuscript were published and the contents made known, authorities in Mexico could ask for you to be deported. You could be arrested for murder, Mrs. Trevor." She shook her head. "I couldn't let that happen."

Thea didn't answer. Tears ran down her cheeks, and she didn't even try to brush them away.

"Don't worry. I'm going to destroy the manuscript, so you're safe now," Mrs. Engstrom told her. Her eyes were dulled with a terrible sadness.

I jabbed at the button near Thea's chair. "I'll get Walter!" I shouted.

Mrs. Engstrom shook her head. "Walter won't hear the bell. He's with Tomás and Lucy, working in the other house."

Thea cried, "What are we going to do, Frances? When the police arrive . . ."

"I'm not worried about the police," Mrs. Engstrom interrupted. "I'm going to take the small boat to the mainland. I'll be gone. The manuscript will be gone." She smiled, and it was so chilling, I shivered.

Thea rose to her feet, releasing me, and I rubbed my hands together, trying to bring back the circulation. "You can't take that little boat into rough seas! You'll be swamped! You won't make it as far as the mainland!"

"I'll take my chances," Mrs. Engstrom said. She turned the manuscript roll on end and caught the handle of a long, sharp kitchen knife that she had hidden inside it. "Come, Miss Burns," she said. "You're going with me."

SEVENTEEN

Thea cried out as Mrs. Engstrom grabbed my arm and propelled me out of the room. The point of the knife was aimed at my neck, and I wasn't about to argue.

As we left the house the wind whipped against us. I clutched the railing to keep from falling, and trotted and skidded down the slippery steps leading to the dock. Even inside the shelter the small motorboat bobbed wildly. Out in the bay, waves leaped and crashed and spit foam, and all I could think about was that we were going to drown.

"I'm not a good swimmer," I told Mrs. Engstrom.

She jerked me around and stared at me with eyes dark with despair. "Why didn't you just leave things alone? Why did you have to pry? Only three of us knew what happened in Acapulco. Now you know too."

"I'm not going to tell anyone."

She waggled the knife toward the ropes that fastened the boat to the dock. "Untie them."

I wrestled with alternatives and made an instant choice. "No," I said.

She blinked with surprise. "Do what I told you," she insisted and waved the knife under my nose.

"I can't. We'd both drown in that boat," I said.

Mrs. Engstrom's face crumpled like wadded paper, and she began to cry. She let go of my arm, and the knife clattered to the dock. "I wouldn't have taken you with me," she said. "I just needed you to untie the boat. I can't work those heavy knots."

She rubbed a hand across her eyes and looked into mine. "You're not in any danger. You're Thea Trevor's niece. Do you think I'd do anything that would hurt her?"

Just to play it safe, I kicked the knife with the side of my shoe. It skittered across the dock and plopped into the water. "Come back into the house with me," I told her. "We can wait there for the police."

Her gaze had shifted to a point far over my left shoulder, and I turned to see what had demanded her attention. In the distance, dipping and rising with the waves, came the police cruiser.

"There's just one thing left to do," Mrs. Engstrom said.

Before I knew what she was up to, she opened the supply chest, pulled out a can of gasoline and a tin box of matches and ran toward the open end of the dock.

"It's windy! You'll set everything on fire!" I shouted at her.

She scowled, but didn't take time to look at me. "Don't you think I know what I'm doing?" she demanded.

She tossed the manuscript to the damp ground, saturated it with the gasoline, and lit the match.

I was right behind her with a bucket I'd used to scoop

up water from the bay, but I held it. I waited until Augustus Trevor's damning manuscript was nothing but a squirming, twisting bundle of glowing ash. That's when I let fly with the water.

The pile sizzled and smelled as most of it slid off the dock into the ocean. A few pieces of the wet ash swirled up into the wind and vanished, and I was satisfied that burning embers weren't going anywhere to cause further damage. Neither were the many personal secrets Augustus had so easily blabbed in print.

I rested a hand on Mrs. Engstrom's arm. "Please believe me," I said. "I'll never tell anyone what I read about Thea." Not even Mom. Not even Darlene. That was a promise I intended to keep forever.

Her expression was dubious, so I added, "And I'll never write about it, either."

Her eyes widened in shock. "Write about it?"

"Yes," I said. "I'm planning to become a writer. I thought I couldn't do it without getting help from Augustus, but I was wrong. I don't know why I thought I needed his opinion. I finally figured out that it's my own opinion that counts."

Mrs. Engstrom gripped my shoulders, her fingertips painfully digging in. For an instant I thought she was going to fling me off the dock into the sea, but instead she pressed close to me, our noses almost touching, and said, "You'll never tell what you read in Mr. Trevor's manuscript! And you won't write about it, either! You promised!"

"I'll keep my promise," I insisted.

Her gaze shifted to the police cruiser, and she whispered to herself, "No more games."

With his mind on his manipulations, his mean little digs and complicated clues, it had never occurred to Augustus Trevor that his terrifying game might draw one player too many. He never had a clue that the name of the game was murder.